I0648169

Abott A Abott

**The Life of Abraham Lincoln**

Abott A Abott

**The Life of Abraham Lincoln**

ISBN/EAN: 9783337414641

Printed in Europe, USA, Canada, Australia, Japan

Cover: Foto ©Raphael Reischuk / pixelio.de

More available books at **www.hansebooks.com**

# THE

# LIFE

## OF

# ABRAHAM LINCOLN.

### BY

## ABOTT A. ABOTT.

Author of " The Statesmen of America," &c.

———————◆———————

NEW YORK:

T. R. DAWLEY, PUBLISHER FOR THE MILLION,

13 AND 15 PARK ROW.

1864.

# THE LIFE

OF

# ABRAHAM LINCOLN.

————————

## CHAPTER I.

### BIRTH AND PARENTAGE.

*Birth and Parentage. A Pioneers Life. Kentucky fifty years Ago. Removed to Indiana. Making Roads. Farm Life. Flat-boating. Removed to Illinois He tends Shop. He grows as tall as a' Pine. Flat-boating again. Grows tired of splitting rails. Off to the Black Hawk War.*

ABRAHAM LINCOLN was born on the 12th of February, 1809, and is now, therefore, past fifty-five years of age.

His parents were Thomas Lincoln, born in Virginia, 1778, and Nancy Hanks, also a Virginian, the date of whose birth is undetermined.

The ancestors of Thomas Lincoln were of English descent, as their name indicates. We find the first traces of them in Pennsylvania, where, as Quakers, their faith naturally led them to settle.

About the year 1780, Abraham Lincoln, the grandfather of the subject of this volume, attracted by the accounts of the lovely and fertile country explored by Daniel Boone, near the Kentucky river, set out with his wife and several young children to find a new home in that vicinity which after gained the name of the "Dark and Bloody Ground."

Lincoln was a frontiers-man, and had for several years previous to his removal to Kentucky, felled the woods and cleared the land which formed his homestead in the Shenandoah Valley of Virginia—that valley since rendered so memorable in the war, which his grandson, the present Abraham, has conducted against the Southern rebels for Union and universal liberty.

Kentucky was at that time a part of the Commonwealth of Virginia, so that in removing even so far away from his former home, Lincoln did not leave the State which had been his home for a time past, and in which his children had been born.

Lincoln's home was somewhere on Floyd's Creek, and probably near its mouth, in what is now Bullitt County, not far distant from the subsequent site of Louisville.

The sanguine hopes he had entertained in regard to the advantages of his new place of residence, were doomed never to be realized. The country was densely covered with pines, and infested with hostile Indians. Its fertility was inferior to that of the fair valley he had left behind him, while his pioneer labors had all to be begun over again. There were possibly other motives which induced his removal than those which proceeded from the hope of gaining a fairer field for his labor—but of these we have heard no mention. If any existed, they most likely arose from the poverty and pecuniary difficulties of the man, and the fondness he shared, with all the colonists of the time, for adventure.

His life was destined never to be passed in Kentucky. He had scarcely marked out his settlement, and commenced to clear it, when he was killed and scalped by an Indian.

His widow thus suddenly bereaved and in a strange land, had now their three sons and two daughters left to her sole protection and care. Fearing to remain in a neighborhood which proved so fatal to their happiness and welfare, this hardy woman removed a few miles further South with her family, to what some eight or ten years afterwards became Washington County. There the soil was more fruitful, and the neighborhood more settled. The family throve apace, and all reached mature age in time. The three sons were named Mordecai, Josiah, and Thomas. The daughters married, one to a man named Crume, the other to one named Bromfield—both backwoodsmen.

In 1792, Kentucky became a separate State. Its population at the time numbered over a hundred thousand souls. This was scarcely thirty years after it was settled by Boone. A period of discontent had followed the formation of the Federal government, caused partly by the inefficiency of the protection afforded by Virginia and the old Federal Congress against the inroad of the savages, and partly by the fear lest the central government should surrender the right to navigate the Mississippi to its mouth. This right of navigation was then shared with France, who owned the territory of Louisiana, and was at that time, owing to the entire absence of railways, or any kind of artificial highways to the sea-board, of the greatest consequence to the interior of the Union.

In 1806, Thomas Lincoln, then twenty-eight years of age, married Nancy Hanks.

Three years afterwards, our hero first came to light in this world of mixed happiness and trouble. His parents were then living in what is now La Rue County, still further South than where the family had removed after grandfather Abraham Lincoln's death. Before Abraham, a girl had been born, who was two years older, and who grew up to womanhood, married, and died—though still young. Two years afterwards Abraham's little brother came into the world, but died in early childhood. Abraham remembers to have visited the grave of this child, along with his mother, before leaving Kentucky.

LaRue county, named from an early settler, John La-Rue, was set off and separately organized in 1843, the portion containing Mr. Lincoln's birthplace having been, up to that date, included in Hardin county. It is a rich grazing country in its more rolling or hilly parts, and the level surface produces good crops of corn and tobacco. In the northern borders of the country, on the Rolling Fork of Salt river, is Muldrow's Hill, a noted eminence. Hodgenville, near which Abraham was born, is a pleasantly situated town on Nolin creek, and a place of considerable business. About a mile above this town, on the creek, is a mound, or knoll, thirty feet above the banks of the stream, containing two acres of level ground, at the top of which there is now a house. Some of the early pioneers encamped on this knoll; and but a short distance from it a fort was erected by Philip Phillips, an emigrrnt from Pennsylvania, about 1780 or 1781, when the elder Lincoln arrived from Virginia. John La Rue came from the latter State with a company of emigrants, and settled, not far from the same date, at Phillips' Fort. Robert Hodgen La Rue's brother-in-law, purchased and occupied the land on which Hodgenville is built.

It is needlest to rehearse the kind of life in which Abraham Lincoln was here trained. The picture is similar in all such settlements. In his case, there was indeed the advantage of a generation or two of progress, since his grandfather had hazarded and lost his life in the then slightly broken wilderness. The State now numbered about 400,000 inhabitants, and had all the benefits of an efficient local administration, the want of which had greatly increased the dangers and difficulties of the first settlers. Henry Clay, it may here be appropriately mentioned, had already, though little more than thirty years of age, begun his brilliant political career, having then served for a year or two in the United States Senate.

Yet with all these changes, the humble laborers, settled near "Hodgen Mills," on Nolin creek, had no other lot but incessant toil, and a constant struggle with nature in the still imperfectly reclaimed wilds, for a plain subsistance. Here the boy spent the first years of his childhood. Before the date of his earliest distinct recollections, he removed with his father to a place six miles distant from Hodgenville, which was ere long to be surrendered, as we shall presently see, for a home in the far-off wilderness, and for frontier life, in its fullest and most significant meaning.

The period of Abraham Lincoln's Kentucky life extends through a little more than seven years, terminating with the autumn of 1816.

In those days there were no common schools in that country, but education was by no meass disregarded, nor did young Lincoln, poor as were his opportunities, grow up an illiterate boy, as some have supposed. Competent teachers were accustomed to offer themselves then, as in later years, who opened private schools for a neighborhood, being supporsed by tuition or subscription. During his boyhood days in Kentucky Abraham Lincoln attended, at different times, at least rwo schools of this description. of which he has clear recollections. One of them was kept by Zacharia Rincy, a Roman Catholic. But although this teacher was himself an ardent Catholic, he made no proselyting efforts in his school. Father Rincy was probably in some way connected with the movement of the " Trappists," who came to Kentucky in the autumn of 1805, and founded an establishment ( abandoned some years later) under Urban Guillet, as superior, on Pottinger's Creek. They were active in promoting education, especially among the poorer classes, and had a school for boys under their immediate supervision. This, however, had been abandoned before the date of Lincoln's first school-days, and it is not improbable that the private schools under Catholic teachers were an offshoot of the original system adopted by these Trappists, who subsequently removed to Illinois.

Another teacher, on whose instructions the boy afterwards attended, while living in Kentucky, was named Caleb Hazel. His was also a neighborhood school, sustained by private patronage.

With the aid of these two schools, and with such further assistance as he received at home, there is no doubt that he had become able to read well, though without having made any great literary progress, at the age of seven. That he was not a dull or inapt scholar, is manifest from his subsequent attainments. With the alluremenes of the rifle and the wild game which then abounded in the country, however, and with the meagre advantages he had, in regard to books, it is certain that his perceptive faculties and his muscular powers, were much more fully developed by exercise than his scholastic talents.

While he lived in Kentucky, he never saw even the exterior of what was properly a church edifice. The religious services he attended were held either at a private dwelling, or in some log school-house.

Unsatisfactory results of these many years' toil on the lands of Nolin Creek, or a restless spirit of adventure and fondness for more genuine pioneer excitements than this region continued to afford, led Thomas Lincoln, now verging on the age of forty, and his son beginning to be of essential service in manual labor, to seek a new place of abode, far to the west, beyond the Ohio river.

Early in the autumn of 1816, Thomas Lincoln determined to pull up stakes as his fathers had done, and emigrate to some new wild. The game was getting scarce, and people began to live uncomfortably near to each other. A backwoodsman can endure a neighbor within twenty miles or so of him, but when they begin to settle any closer, he feels too much crowded, and moves away to lonelier wilds.

Crossing the Ohio, then called the Beautiful River by the Indians, in an emigrant's wagon, the mother and daughter huddled with their beds and household utensils in the body of the vehicle, the father driving the jaded team, and the stripling keeping the indispensable cow up to her proper pace, his adventurous family safely reached the Indiana shore by means of a raft. They landed at the mouth of Anderson's Creek, about 140 miles below Louis-ville, by the river, but hardly 100 miles from their former "clearing."

Here their difficulties began. They were destined to a point near the present town of Ventryville, some twenty miles back from the river. The whole intermediate distance was a dense forest. There was no help for it; the road had to be cut through with the axe.

The story goes that Thomas sold his farm in Kentucky for a lot of whiskey, but we can find no substantial evidence for this version. His whiskey is said to have been lost while crossing the Ohio. But we discredit the entire tale.

In a week's time the arduous journey was performed, and the big-fisted Kentuckian had the satisfaction of reaching the scene of his future hopes without any further accident. During this period the lanky young Abraham, shoeless and hatless, made himself generally useful in
A pair of breeches a world too wide for his shrunken shanks.

These breeches, reaching nearly to his neck, were supported by a single short strap over his shoulder, and with a checked shirt which the owner had neglected to send to the laundry for a long time, made up the entire costume of the future president of the United States.

Fortune plays queer tricks with us all, but she never committed a more extraordinary freak than when she made this little ragged urchin the chief magistrate of a great nation.

Indiana, at this date, was still a Territory, having been originally united under the same government with Illinois, after the admission of Ohio as a State, "the first-born of the great North-west," 1802. A separate territorial organization was made for each in 1809. A few months before the arrival of Thomas Lincoln, namely, in June, 1816, pursuant to a Congressional "enabling act," a Convention had been held which adopted a State Constitution, preparatory to admission into the Union. Under this Constitution, a month or two later, in December, 1816, Indiana became, by act of Congress, a sovereign State.

The next thirteen years Abraham Lincoln spent here, in Southern Indiana, near the Ohio, nearly midway between Louisville and Evansville. He was now old enough to begin to take an active part in the farm labors of his father, and he manfully performed his share of hard work. He learned to use the axe and to hold the plough. He became inured to all the duties of seed-time and harvest. On many a day, during every one of those thirteen years, this Kentucky boy might have been seen with a long "gad" in his hand, driving his father's team in the field, or from the woods with a heavy draught, or on the rough path to the mill, the store, or the river-landing.

A vigorous constitution, and a cheerful, unrepining disposition, made all his labors comparatively light. To such a one, this sort of life has in it much of pleasant excitement to compensate for its hardships. He learned to derive enjoyment from the severest lot.

At occasional intervals Abraham derived instruction in the rudiments from the school teachers of the neighborhood. A Mr. Crawford had one, and a Mr. Dorsey another.

That we may estimate Mr. Lincoln in his true character, as chiefly a self-educated man, it should be stated that, summing up all the days of his actual attendance upon school instruction, the amount would hardly exceed one year. The rest he had accomplished for himself in his own way. As a youth he read with avidity such instructive works as he could obtain, and in winter evenings read them by the mere light of the blazing fire-place, when no better resource was at hand.

An incident having its appropriate connection here, and illustrating several traits of the man, as already developed in early boyhood, is vouched for by a citizen of Evansville, who knew him in the days referred to. In his eagerness to acquire knowldege, young Lincoln had borrowed of Mr. Crawford a copy of Weems' Life of Washington—the only one known to be in existence in the neighborhood. Before he had finished reading the book, it had been left, by a not unnatural oversight, in a window. Meantime, a rain storm came on, and the book was so thoroughly wet as to make it nearly worthless. This mishap caused him much pain ; but he went, in all honesty, to Crawford, with the rained book, explained the calamity that had happened through his neglect, and offered, not having sufficient money, to "work out" the value of the book.

" Well, Abe," said Crawford, "as it's you I won't be hard on you. Come over and pull fodder for me for two days, and we will call our accounts even."

The offer was accepted and the engagement literally fulfilled.

The book was of course worth the labor. There is therefore nothing to be admired in the way of generosity. But the honorable part of the incident lies in the quick acknowledgment of the injury Abraham had caused to the book, and the eagerness he displayed to furnish an equivalent for it to its owner.

At the age of nineteen, Abraham, tired of the farm and longing for adventure, with an eye, too, to profit, tried his hand at flat-boating. He sailed down the Ohio and the Mississippi on a raft, doing service as one of the laborers. Naturally lively and fond of a joke, the vocation rather improved his faculties of humor. He worked, sang, danced, cracked jokes, wrestled, fished, cooked his own meals, and made himself agreeable and loveable with all. The incidents of this voyage to New Orleans and back have since formed the groundwork for many of the statesman's sallies of wit.

If there had been any forebodings at the time of departure from their first home on Nolin Creek, these were to be ere-long realized by the Indiana emigrants. Scarcely two years had passed, in this changed climate, and in these rougher forest experiences, before the mother of young Abraham was called to a last seperation from those she had so tenderly loved. She died in 1818, leaving as her sole surviving chi'dren, a daughter less than twelve years old, and a son two years younger, of whose future distinction, the humble son probably never had the remotest dr am. A year later, Thomas Lincoln married another wife, a Mrs. Johnston. This person was a widow with three chi'dren, all of whom were adopted by their step-father and became members of the family.

Abraham's life upon his return from New Orleans, and was before—the life of a farm boy, laborious and eventless.

Thus it was that he grew up to the verge of manhood; he led no idle or enervating existence. Accustomed to steady labor, no one of all the workingmen with with whom he came in contact was a better sample of his class than he. He had now become a Saul among the pioneers, having reached the height of nearly six feet and four inches, and with a c mparatively slender yet uncommonly strong, and muscular frame.

In the spring of 1830, Thomas L'ncoln resolved to emigrate once more. His brother had previously removed to more northern locations in Indiana. This, and his fondness for change, and the hope of better fortune, induced him to leave the hills of Indiana for the flat prairie lands of Illinois. Mordecai had died in Hancock County. Josiah still lived in Hamilton County.

The journey was accomplished in fifteen days. The spot selected was on the north side of Sangamon River.

Illinois had but just begun to be occupied, and only along the banks of the principle streams, in order to secure the advantages of wood and water, with both of which the interior of the State is but poorly supplied.

Assisted by a man name John Hunter, Abraham was deputed to split the rails for fencing the new farm. These are the rails about which so much was said in the late Presidential campaign. "Their existence," says Mr. Scripps, " was brought to the public attention during the sitting of the Republican State Convention, at Decatur, on which occasion a banner, attached to two of these rails, and bearing an appropriate inscription was brought into the assemblage and formally presented to that body, amid a scene of unparalleled enthusiasm. After that they were in demand in every State of the Union in which free labor is honored, where they were borne in processions of the people, and hailed by hundreds of thousands of freemen, as a symbol of triumph, and as a glorious vindication of freedom, and of the rights and the dignity of free labor· These, however, were far from being the first or only rails made by Lincoln. He was a practised hand at the business. His first lessons were taken while yet a boy in Indiana.

For some unexplained reason, the family did not remain on this place but a single year. Abraham was now of age, and when, in the spring of 1831, his father set out for Coles county, sixty or seventy miles to the eastward, on the upper waters of the Kaskaskia and Embarras, a separ-

ation took place, the son for the first time assuming his
independence, and commencing life on his own account.
The scene of these labors he has not since visited. His
father was soon after comfortably settled in the place to
which he had turned his course, and spent the remainder
of his adventurous days there, arriving at a good old age.
He died in Coles county, on the 17th day of January,
1851, being in his seventy-third year. The farm on the
Sangamon subsequently came into the possession of a man
named Whitley, who also erected a mill in the vicinity.

While there was snow on the ground, at the close of the
year 1830 or early in 1831, a man came to that part of
Macon county where young Lincoln was living, in pursuit of hands to aid him in a flat-boat voyage down the
Mississippi. The fact was known that the youth had once
made such a trip, and his services were sought for the occasion. As one who had his own subsistence to earn,
with no capital but his hands, and with no immediate opportunities for commencing professional study, if his
thoughts had as yet been turned in that direction, he accepted the proposition made him. Perhaps there was
something of his inherited and acquired fondness for exciting adventure, impelling him to this decision. With
him, were also employed, his former fellow-laborer, John
Hanks, and a son of his step-mother, named John Johnson. In the spring of 1831, Lincoln set out to fulfill his
engagement. The floods had so swollen the streams that
the Sangamon country was a vast sea before. His first
entrance into that country was over these wide-spread
waters, in a canoe. The time had come to join his em-

ployer on his journey to New Orleans, but the latter had been disappointed by another person on whom he relied to furnish him a boat, on the Illinois river. Accordingly, all hands set to work and themselves built a boat, on that river for their purposes. This done, they set out on their long trip, making a successful voyage to New Orleans and back. It is reported by his friends, that Mr. Lincoln refers with much pleasant humor to this early experience' so relating some of its incidents as to afford abundant amusement to his auditors. In truth, he was a youth who could adapt himself to this or any other honest work, which his circumstances required of him, and with a cheerfulness and alacrity—a certain practical humor—rarely equalled. He could turn off the hardest labor as a mere pastime; and his manly presence, to other laborers, was as a constant' inspiration and a charm to lighten their burdens.

It was midsummer when the flat-boatman returned from this, his second and last trip, in that capacity. The man who had commanded this little expedition now undertook to establish himself in business at New Salem, twenty miles below Springfield, in Menard county—a place of more relative consequence then than now—two miles from Petersburg, the county seat. He had found young Lincoln a person of such sort that he was anxious to secure his services in the new enterprise he was about to embark in. He opened a store at New Salem, and also a mill for flouring grain. For want of other immediate employment, and in the same spirit which had heretofore actuated him, Abraham Lincoln now entered upon the

duties of a clerk, having an eye to both branches of the
business carried on by his employer. This connection
lasted for nearly a year, all the duties of his position being
faithfully and cheerfully performed.                    ' .

Some how or other this country grocer did not succeed,
and the Black Hawk War breaking out about this time,
young Lincoln, always ready for adventure, left the shop,
and volunteered for service against the Indians.

## CHAPTER II.

### THE VOLUNTEER.

*Breaking out of the Black Hawk War. Lincoln volunteers. He is
chosen Captain. Vicisitudes of the campaign. Battle of the Bad-Axe.
End of the volunteers first campaign.*

IN the spring of 1831, Black Hawk, unmindful of his
treaty to remain west of the Mississippi, and charging bad
faith upon the whites, re-crossed the river with all his
tribe, the women and children included, and sought to return to his old hunting-grounds in the Rock river country. He was assisted by allies from the Kickapoo and
Pottawatomie tribes. These, with the Sacs, made up a
force of some three hundred fighting men.

At this time Abraham Lincoln was clerking it in the
'store" in Menard county.

In response to the representations of Gov. Reynolds, to
whom the settlers applied for protection, Gen. Gaines,
commander of the United States forces in that quarter,
took prompt and decisive measures to expel these invaders

from the State. With a few companies of regular soldiers, Gen. Gaines at once took up his position at Rock Island, and at his call, several hundred volunteers, assembled from the northern and central parts of the State, upon the proclamation of Gov. Reynold's, joined him a month later. His little army, distributed into two regiments, an additional batalion, and a spy batalion, was the most formidable military force yet seen in the new State. The expected battle did not take place, the Indians having suddenly and stealthily retired again, in their canoes, across the river. The troops had been advanced to Vandruff's Island, opposite the Indian town, where the engagement was anticipated, and there was much dissatisfaction among the volunteers, and some complaints against the generals, Gaines and Duncan for permitting the enemy to escape.

Negotiations soon followed. It was sought to restrain Black Hawk from ever again crossing the river. Threats and promises were freely used, and for a time both had the effect intended. A treaty was entered into by which the chief agreed that he and his tribe should ever after remain on the west side of the river, unless by permission of the State Governor, or of the President. Thus was the treaty of 1804 reaffirmed, by which the lands they were claiming had been distinctly conveyed to the United States Government, which, in turn, had sold them to the present settlers.

In express violation, however, of this second deliberate engagement, Black Hawk and his followers began, early in the spring of 1832, to make preparations for another

invasion. Many and grevious wrongs have undoubtedly
been inflicted upon the savage tribes, by the superior race
that has gradually, but steadily driven the former from
their ancient homes. But the bad faith shown in this
case, and the repeated violation of deliberate agreements,
was wholly without justification or excuse. No provica-
tion or plausible pretext had arisen after the treaty of the
previous June; yet Black Hawk, under the misguided influence and false representations of the "Prophet," who
persuaded him to believe that the British (to whom Black
Hawk had always been a fast friend), as well as the Otta-
was, Chippewas, Winnebagoes and Pottowatomies would
aid them in regaining their village and the adjoining.
lands. Under this delusion, to which the wiser Keokuk
refused to become a dupe, though earnestly invited to
join them, Black Hawk proceeded to gather as strong a
force as possible. He first established his headquarters at
the old site of fort Madison, west of the Mississippi.
After his preparations had been complete l, he proceeded up the river with his women and children, his property
and camp equipage, in canoes, while his warrior armed
and mounted, advanced by land. In spite of a warning
he had received that there was a stroug force of white
soldiers at Fort Armstrong, on Rock Island, he continued
on to the mouth of Rock river, where, in utter reckless-
ness and bad faith—paying not the slightest regard to his
solemn agreement of the last year—the whole party
crossed to the east side of the Mississippi, with a declared
purpose of ascending Rock river to the territory of the
Winnebagoes. This was in the early part of April, 1822.

Black Hawk, after he had gone some distance up this river, was overtaken by a messenger from Gen. Atkinson, who had command of the troops on Rock Island, and ordered to return beyond the Mississippi. This was defiantly refused.

Gov. Reynolds again issued a call for volunteers to protect the settlers from this invasion. A company was promptly raised in Menard county, in the formation of which, Abraham Lincoln was one of the most active. From New Salem, Clary's Grove, and elswhere in the vicinity, an efficient force was gathered, and in making their organization, Lincoln was elected captain.

They first marched to Beardstown. Here 1800 men were speedily assembled and organized into four regiments, with an additional spy battalion. Gen. Sam. Whiteside was in command. Gen. James D. Henry was placed at the head of the spy battalion.

On the 27th of April they left Beardstown and marched to Oquawka, and thence to the mouth of Rock river. After marching fifty miles up the river they arrived at the Prophet's village, which they left in flames, and then pushed forward to Dixon's Ferry, forty miles further up, where the Indians were supposed to be. On the way they were joined by 275 more men from McLean, Pecona and other counties.

On the 12th of May their advance guard skirmished with, and killed three Indians. Black Hawk, his skirmishers, and the whites did the same. In a short time the engagement employed some five hundred men from each side. It resulted in a complete rout of the whites, and is known to day as the unfortunate affair of "Stillman's Defeat."

A council of war was held, and it was determined to renew the battle the next morning, but when the whtes arrived at the scene of action the wiley savages had disappeared.

After this attempt to fall in with the enemy and give him battle, Gen. Whiteside, having buried the dead of the day before, returned to camp, where he was joined, next day, by Gen. Atkinson, with his troops and supplies. The numbers of the army were thus increased to twenty-four hundred, and a few weeks more would have enabled this force to bring the war to a successful close. But many of the volunteers, whose time had nearly expired, were eager to be discharged. They had seen quite enough of the hardships of a campaign, which, without bringing as yet any glory, had turned out in reality quite different from what their imagination had foretold. With the prevailing discontents, but one course was possible. The volunteers were marched to Ottawa, where they were discharged by Gov. Reynolds, on the 27th and 28th of May.

Gov. Reynolds had previously issued a call for two thousand new volunteers to assemble at Beardstown and Hennepin. In accordance with the wishes of Lincoln and others, who were still ready to bear their share of the campaign to its close, the Governor also asked for the formation of a volunteer regiment from those just discharged. Lincoln promptly enrolled himself as a private, as did also General Whiteside.

Before the arrival of the other levies, a skirmishing

fight with the Indians was had at Burr Oak Grove, on the 18th of June, in which the enemy was defeated, with considerable loss, and on the side of the volunteers, two killed and one wounded.

The whites now numbered 3200 volunteers and a force of regulars under Gen. Atkinson, of the regular army.

Meanwhile, Black Hawk had concentrated his forces at the Four Lakes, tired of being hunted down, and resolved to try the issue of the war in a general engagement. But some how or other, the whites never succeeded in finding their enemy.

Nearly two months had now passed since the opening of the campaign, and its purpose seemed as remote from accomplishment as ever. The new volunteers had many of them become discontented, like the former ones. Their number had in fact become reduced one-half. The wearisome marches, the delays, the privations and exposures, had proved to them that this service was no pastime, and that its romance was not what it seemed in the distance. They sickened of such service, and were glad to escape from its restraints. Not so, however, with Lincoln, who had found in reality the kind of exciting adventure which his spirit craved. While others murmured and took their departure, he remained true and persistent, no less eager for the fray, or ambitious to play a genuine soldier's part, than at the beginning. To him it had been what his imagination painted, and he had a hearty earnestness in his work that kept him cheerful, and strongly attached others to him.

Just here Abraham Lincoln's campaign ended. He was

not destined to share in any encounter with the enemy beyond what we have already mentioned. The forces were divided and dispersed, and one portion shortly after meeting with the Indians, a battle ensued, and the war was over. This will be related in a few words:

Two days after their separation news was received by that portion of the whites from which Lincoln's company had been separated that Black Hawk was thirty miles above their camp on Rock river. A plan of Generals Alexander, Henry, and others, to take him by surprise, without awaiting orders, was frustrated by their troops refusing to follow them. Gen. Henry finally set out in pursuit of the Indians, on the 15th of July, but was misled by treachery. He continued on for several days, acquiring better information, passing the beautiful country around the Four Lakes, the present site of Madison, Wisconsin, and after another day's hard march came close upon the retreating Indians, and finally overtook them on the 21st. They were immediately charged upon, and driven along the high bluffs of the Wisconsin, and down upon the river bottom. The Indians lost sixty-eight killed, and of the large number wounded twenty-five were afterwards found dead on their trail leading to the Mississippi. The regulars, in this engagement on the Wisconsin, were commanded by Gen. (then Col.) Zachary Taylor, afterward President of the United States. Gen. Henry, of Illinois, and Col. Dodge, (afterward United States Senator), were chief commanders of the volunteers.

Waiting two days at the Blue Mounds, the forces still in the field were all united, and a hard pursuit resumed through the forests, down the Wisconsin. On the fourth day, they reached the Mississippi, which some of the Indians had already crossed, while others were preparing to do so. The battle of the Bad-Ax here brought the war to a close, with the capture of Black Hawk and his surviving warriors.

Lincoln never set up any claims to heroism in this, his only campaign as a soldier, but he believed he did his duty, and so did others. Perhaps if he had the opportunity he might have turned out quite a redoubtable warrior; but it was all for the best, for he might have been diverted from that career of usefulness which he afterwards pursued in quieter ways.

Sarcastically commenting on the efforts of Gen. Cass's biographers to make the old Statesman a military hero, Lincoln, in a congressional speech, delivered during the canvas of 1848, said :

"By the way, Mr. Speaker, did you know I am a military hero ? Yes, sir, in the days of the Black Hawk war, I fought, bled, and came away. Speaking of Gen. Cass's career, reminds me of my own. I was not at Stillman's defeat, but I was about as near it as Cass to Hull's surrender; and like him, I saw the place very soon afterward."

This never failing humor of Abraham Lincoln, no doubt has done as much as anything to make him a general favorite. It is said that a man that is fond of music can never be a conspirator or a traitor. We might extend the rule, and say, that one who is always good natured and humorous, is alike incapable of double dealing or plotting.

At least, so think the multitude, and they are not often wrong.

Whether it was this characteristic, so highly prized among our countrymen, or the scrupulous honesty which attacoed itself to allof the young pioneer's dealings, we do not know but Abraham Lincoln at this time came to be called Honest Abe. It is a good sign for him when a man earns this handle to his name, and is a sure forerunner of fortune and honor.

---

## CHAPTER III.

### THE POLITICIAN.

*Abraham becomes a politician: Takes to surveying. Sells his instruments at auction. Studies law. Is beaten at an election. Runs again and succeeds. Elected four times to the legislature. Stumps the State for Henry Clay. His oratorical powers. His appearance and personal habits.*

After his return from the Black Hawk War, Abraham began to cast about him for something to do. His military campaign had infused that self-confidence within him to which he had hitherto been a stranger. Chosen as captain above a hundred of his fellows, it would be strange if the youth did not begin to have some aspirations for distinction in life. He accordingly began to make himself acquainted with the political machinery of elections and to study the complexions of parties, and take his position among them according to the opinions he held.

Lincoln was an ardent admirer of the then newly famous Henry Clay of Kentucky, and it took him but little time to enrol himself among his numerous followers and oppose the Democratic party, who at that time advocated Gen. Jackson for the presidency.

In 1834 he ran for the Illinois legislature, but was defeated.

Meanwhile, he pursued the business of land surveyor, as Washington had done before him, but with such little success that he was at one time compelled to sell his surveying instruments at auction in order to keep soul and body together. He was at the same time studying law, and his abandonment of surveying only made him more anxious to succeed with his books and his degree. His political aspirations were not without success even then, for in consequence of his popularity on the occasion of his defeat, (lacking only seven votes of election) he received the appointment of postmaster at New Salem, Illinois.

In 1836 he ran again for the legislature, and this time was successful. In 1838 and 1840 he was re-elected to the same office.

During this part of his career as a politician, it is interesting to notice the care he took even when a young man to avoid identifying himself with the theoretical abolitionists of the day, and yet to place himself on the record as a firm lover of liberty for all men when time and circumstances favored emancipation measures.

During the spring of 1837, revolutions of a pro-slavery character had been adopted by the majority of the Illinois legislature. These of course would have affixed the character of theoretical abolitionists to those who voted against them. In order to extricate himself from a posi-

tion which he at that time considered unwise, he joined
with a Mr. Stone in the following protest on the subject:

MARCH 3d, 1837.

The following protest was presented to the House,
which was read and ordered to be spread on the jouanais,
to wit :

" Resolutions upon the subject of domestic slavery having passed both branches of the General Assembly, at its
present session, the undersigned hereby protest against
the passage of the same.

" They believe that the institution of slavery is founded
on both injustice and bad policy ; but that the promulga-
tion of abolition doctrines tends rather to increase than
abate its evils.

" They believe that the Congress of the United States
has no power, under the Constitution, to interfere with
the institution of slavery in the different States.

" They believe that the Congress of the United States
has the power, under the Constitution, to abolish slavery
in the District of Columbia ; but that the power ought not
to be exercised, unless at the request of the people of said
District.

" The difference between these opinions and those contained in the said resolutions, is their reason for entering
this protest.

" (Signed)

" DAN. STONE,<br>
" A. LINCOLN,<br>
" <i>Representatives from the County of Sangamon.</i>"</div>

In 1836, he had obtained a license to practice law, and in April, 1837, removed to Springfield and opened a law office, in partnership with Major John F. Stuart. He rose rapidly to distinction in the profession, and was especially eminent as an advocate in jury trials, in consequence of the rare power he possessed of making himself understood by his auditors, and appealing to their sense of fairness and justice in the cause he represented.

This quality as an orator he has ever wielded with success, and in fact has been the corner-stone of his advancement and elevation.

We trust the example thus afforded to American youth will not be lost upon them. There is no accomplishment capable of yielding so rich a return in this land of democracy and popular freedom, than that one which makes us the exponent, the mouth-pieces, and afterwards the advocate and leader of the masses.

After Abraham Lincoln's repeated service in the legislature of his adopted State, he was several times a candidate for Presidential elector, and as such in 1844 he canvassed the entire State, together with part of Indiana, in behalf of Henry Clay, making almost daily speeches to large audiences.

At this time he was very plain in his costume, as well as rather uncourtly in his address and general appearance. His clothing was of homely Kentucky jean, and the first impression made by his tall, lank figure, upon those who saw him was not specially prepossessing. He had not outgrown his hard backwoods experience, and showed no inclination to disguise or to cast behind him the honest and man y, though unpolished characteristics of his earlier days. Never was a man further removed from all snobbish affectation. As little was there, also, of the demagogue art of assuming an uncouthness or rusticity of manner and outward habit, with the mistaken notion of thus securing particular favor as one of the masses. He chose to appear then, as he has at all times since, precisely what he was. His deportment was unassuming, without any awkwardness of reserve.

First elected at twenty-five, he had continued in office without interruption so long as his inclination allowed, and until, by his uniform courtesy and kindness of manners, his marked ability, and his straight-forward integrity, he had won an enviable repute throughout the State, and was virtually, when but a little past thirty, placed at the head of his party in Illinois.

Begun in comparative obscuaity, and without any adventitious aids in its progress, this period of his life, at its termination, had brought him to a position where he was secure in the confidence of the people, and prepared, in due time, to enter upon a more enlarged and brilliant career, as a national statesman. His fame as a close and convincing debater was established. His native talent as an orator had at once been demonstrated and disciplined. His zeal and earnestness in behalf of a party whose principles he believed to be right, had rallied strong troops of political friends about him, while his unfeigned modesty and his unpretending and simple bearing, in marked contrast with that of so many imperious leaders, had won him general and lasting esteem. He preferred no claim as a partisan, and showed no overweening anxiety to advance himself, but was always a disinterested and generous co-worker with his associates, only ready to accept the post of honor and of responsibility when it was clearly their will, and satisfactory to the people whose interests were involved. At the close of this period, with scarcely any consciousness of the fact himself, and with no noisy demonstrations or flashy ostentations in his behalf from his friends, he was really one of the foremost political men in the State. A keen observer might even then have predicted a great future for the " Sangamon Chief," as people have been wont to call him ; and only such an observer, perhaps, would then have adequately estimated his real power as a natural orator, a sagacious statesman, and a gallant TRIBUNE OF THE PEOPLE.

The following incident, of which the narration is believed to be substantially accurate, is from the pen of one who professes to write from personal knowledge. It is given in this connection, as at once illustrating the earlier struggles of Mr. Lincoln in acquiring his profession, the character of his forensic efforts, and the generous gratitude and disinterestedness of his nature :

Having chosen the law as his future calling, he devoted himself assiduously to its mastery, contending at every step with adverse fortune. During this period of study, he for some time found a home under the hospitable roof of one Armstrong, a farmer, who lived in a log house some eight miles from the village of Petersburg, in Menard county. Here, young Lincoln would master his lessons by the firelight of the cabin, and then walk to town for the purpose of recitation. This man Armstrong was himself poor, but he saw the genuis struggling in the young student, and opened to him his rude home, and bid him welcome to his rude fare. How Lincoln graduated with promise—how he has more than fulfilled that promise—how honorably he acquitted himself, alike on the battlefield, in defending our border settlements against the ravages of savage foes, and in the halls of our national legislature, are matters of history, and need no repetition here. But one little incident of a more private nature, standing as it does as a sort of sequel to some things already alluded to, I deem worthy of record. Some few years since, the oldest son of Mr. Lincoln's old friend Armstrong, the chief support of his widowed mother—the good old man having some time previously passed from earth—was arrested on the charge of murder. A young man had been killed during a riotous melee, in the night-time, at a camp-meeting, and one of his associates stated that the death-wound was inflicted by young Armstrong. A preliminary examination was gone into, at which the accuser testified so positively, that there seemed no doubt of the guilt of the prisoner, and therefore he was held for trial. As is too often the case, the bloody act caused an undue degree of excitement in the public mind. Every improper incident in the life of the prisoner—each act which bore the least semblance of rowdyism—each school-boy quarrel—was suddenly remembered and magnified, until they pictured him as a fiend of the most horrid hue. As these rumors spread abroad, they were received as gospel truth, and a feverish desire for vengeance seized upon the infatuated populace, while only prison-bars prevented a horrible death at the hands of the mob. The events were heralded in the newspapers, painted in highest colors, accompanied by rejoicing over the certainty of punishment being meted out to the guilty party. The prisoner, overwhelmed by the circumstances in which he found himself placed fell into a melancholy condition, bordering upon despair; and the widowed mother, lo king through her tears, saw no cause for hope from earthly aid.

At this juncture, the widow received a letter from Mr. Lincol , volunteering his serv'ces in an effort to save the youth from the impending stroke. Gladly was his aid accepted, although it seemed impossible for even his sagacity to prevail in such a desperate case; but the heart of the attorney was in his work, and he set about it with a will that knew no such word as fail. Feeling that the poisoned condition of the public mind was such as to preclude the possibility of impanneling an impartial jury in the court having jurisdiction, he procured a change of venue, and a postponement of the trial. He then went studiously to work unraveling the history of the case, and satisfied himself that his client was the victim of malice, and that the statements of the accuser were a tissue of falsehoods. When the trial was called on, the prisoner, pale and emaciated, with hopelessness written on every feature, and accompanied by his half-hoping, half-despairing mother—whose only hope was in a mother's belief of her son's innocence, in the justice of the God she worshiped, and in the noble counsel, who, without hope of fee or reward upon earth, had undertaking the cause—took his seat in the prisoner's box, and with a " stony firmness" listened to the reading of the indictment.

Lincoln sat quietly by, while the large auditory looked on him as though wondering what he could say in defense of one whose guilt they regarded as certain. The examination of the witnesses for the State was begun, and a well-arranged mass of evidence, circumstantial and positive, was introduced, which seemed to impale the prisoner beyond the possibility of extrication. The counsel for the defense propounded but few questions, and those of a character which excited no uneasiness on the part of the prosecutor—merely, in most cases, requiring the main witness to be definite as to time and place. When the evidence of the prosecution was ended, Lincoln introduced a few witnesses to remove some erroneous impressions in regard to the previous character of his client, who, though somewhat rowdyish, had never been known to commit a vicious act; and to show that a greater degree of ill-feeling existed between the accuser and accused, than the accused and the deceased. The prosecutor felt that the case was a clear one, and his opening speech was brief an ! formal. Lincoln arose, while a deathly silence pervaded the vast audience, and in a clear but moderate tone began his argument. Slowly and carefully he reviewed the testimony, pointing out the hitherto unobserved discrepancies in the statements of the principal witness. That which had seemed plain and plausible, he made to appear crooked as a serpent's path. The witness had stated that the affair took place at a certain hour in the evening, and

that, by the aid of the brightly shining moon. he saw the
prisoner inflict the death-blow with a slung shot. Mr.
Lincoln showed that, at the hour referred to, the moon had
not yet appeared above the horizon, and consequently the
whole tale was a fabrication. An almost instantaneous
change seemed to have been wrought in the minds of his
auditors, and the verdict of "not guilty" was at the end
of every tongue. But the advocate was not content with
this intellectual achievement. His whole being had for
months been bound up in this work of gratitude and
mercy, and, as the lava of the overcharged crater bursts
from its imprisonment, so great thoughts and burning
words leaped forth from the soul of the eloquent Lincoln.
He drew a picture of the perjurer, so horrid and ghastly,
that the accuser could sit under it no longer, but reeled
and staggered from the court-room, while the audience
fancied they could see the brand upon his brow. Then, in
words of thrilling pathos, Lincoln appealed to the jurors,
as fathers of sons who might become fatherless, and as
husbands of wives who might be widows, to yield to no
previous impressions, no ill-founded prejudice, but to do
his client justice ; and as he alluded to the debt of gratitude which he owed the boy's sire, tears were seen to fall
from many eyes unused to weep. It was near night when
he concluded by saying, that if justice was done—as he
believed it would be—before the sun should set, it would
shine upon his client a freeman. The jury retired, and
the court adjourned for the day. Half an hour had not
elapsed, when, as the officers of the court and the volunteer attorney sat at the tea-table of their hotel, a messen-

ger announced that the jury had returned to their seats. All repaired immediately to the court-house, and while the prisoner was being brought from the jail, the court-room was filled to overflowing with citizens of the town. When the prisoner and his mother entered, silence reigned as completely as though the house were empty. The foreman of the jury, in answer to the usual inquiry from the court, delivered the verdict "Not guilty!" The widow dropped into the arms of her son, who lifted her up, and told her to look upon him as before, free and innocent. Then, with the words, "Where is Mr. Liocoln?" he rushed across the room and grasped the hand of his deliverer, while his heart was too full for utterance. Lincoln turned his eyes toward the west, where the sun still lingered in view, and then, turning to the youth, said, "It is not yet sundown, and you are free." I confess that my cheeks were not wholly unwet by tears, and I turned from the affecting scene. As I cast a glance behind, I saw Abraham Lincoln obeying the divine injunction, by comforting the widow and the fatherless.

## CHAPTER IV.

### THE STATESMAN.

*Mr Lincoln's Marriage. Election to Congress. His firsh Speech in the House. Pertinent Extracts. War. Subjugation. Right of Revolution. Indemnity. Peace. Confiscation. The Model President. Platforms. One of Honest Abe's Jokes. The Scathing and Withering style. The great Democratic Ox-gad. How much a man may Sub. Visit to New England. Retires to Private Life. The Kansas Bill rouses him. He takes the field again. Campaign for Fremont. The Principles of the Republican Party. Debates with Judge Douglass. The Campaign of 1858. Shooting over the line. The Kentucky Girls. The Speech to the Children in New York. Nomination to the Presidency. What Douglass said of his color. The Campaign of 1860.*

On the 4th of November 1842, Mr. Lincoln was married to Miss Mary Todd, daughter of Hon. Robert S. Todd of Lexington, Kentucky.

A man of family, a recognised leader in the ranks of the Whig party, a successful lawyer, and one whose popularity was daily increasing, it is not a matter of wonder that in 1848 Mr. Lincoln's fellow citizens should have deemed him an appropriate man to represent them in the National Congress.

Accordingly he was returned for the central district of Illinois in the Fall of 1846, and took his seat in the house of Representatives at Washington, on the 6th day of December, 1847, the opening of the thirtieth Congress.

Mr. Lincoln was comparatively quite a young man when he entered the House, yet he was early recognised as one of the foremost of the Western men on the floor. His Congressional record, throughout, is that of a Whig of those days, his votes on all leading national subjects, beind invariably what those of Clay, Webster or Corwin would have been, had they occupied his place. One of the most prominent subjects of consideration before the Thirtieth Congress, very naturally, was the then existing war with Mexico. Mr. Lincoln was one of those who believed the Administration had not properly managed its affairs with Mexico at the outset, and who, while voting supplies and for suitably rewarding our gallant soldiers in that war, were unwilling to be forced, by any trick of the supporters of the Administration, into an unqualified indorsement of its course in this affair, from beginning to end. In this attitude, Mr. Lincoln did not stand alone. Such was the position of Whig members in both Houses, without exception.

On the 12th of January, 1848, he made his speech in the House, from which we make the following extracts as being pertinent to the issues which at present divide the country :

*(In Committee of the Whole House, January 12, 1848.)*

Mr. Lincoln addressed the Committee as follows :

Mr. Chairman ; Some, if not all, of the gentlemen on the other side of the House, who have addressed the Committee within the last two days, have spoken rather complainingly, if I have rightly understood them, of the vote given a week or ten days ago, declaring that the war with Mexico was unnecessarily and unconstitutionally commenced by the President. I admit that such a vote should not be given in mere party wantonness, and that the one given is justly censurable. if it have no other or better foundation. I am one of those who joined in that vote; and did so under my best impression of the *truth* of the case. How I got this impression, and how it may possibly be removed, I will now try to show. When the war began, it was my opinion that all those who, because of knowing too *little*, or because of knowing too *much*, could not conscientiously approve the conduct of the President (in the beginning of it), should, nevertheless, as good citizens and patriots, remain silent on that point, at least till the war should be ended. Some leading democrats, including ex-President Van Buren, have taken this same view, as I understand them; and I adhered to it, and acted upon it, until since I took my seat here; and I think I should still adhere to it, were it not that the President and his friends will not allow it to be so. Besides, the continual effort of the President to argue every silent vote given for supplies into an endorsement of the justice and wisdom of his conduct; besides that singularly candid paragraph in his late message, in which he tells us that Congress, with great unanimity (only two in the Senate and fourteen in the House dissenting) had declared that "by the act of the Republic of Mexico a state of war exists between that Government and the United States;" when the same journals that informed him of this, also informed that, when that declaration stood disconnected from the question of supplies, sixty-seven in the House, and not fourteen, merely, voted against it; besides this open attempt to prove by telling the *truth*, what he could not prove by telling the *whole truth*, demanding of all who will not submit to be misrepresented, in justice to themselves, to speak out; besides all this, one of my colleagues [Mr. Richardson], at a very early day in the session, brought n a set of resolutio ns expressly endorsing the original ju s tice of the war on the part of the President. Upon these resolutions, when they shall be put on their passage, I shall be *compelled* to vote; so that I cannot be silent if I would. Seeing this, I went about preparing myself to give the vote understandingly, when it should come. I carefully examined the President's messages, to ascertain what he himself had said and proved upon the point. The result of this examination was to make the impression, that, taking for true all the President states as facts, he falls far short of proving his justification; and the President would have gone further with his proof, if it had not been for the small matter that the *truth* would not permit him. Under the impression thus made I gave the vote before mentioned. I propose now to give, concisely, the process of the examination I made, and how I reached the conclusion I did.

Any people anywhere, being inclined and HAVING THE POWER, have a *right* to rise up and shake off the existing government, and form a new one that suits them better. This is a most valuable, a most sacred right—a right which, we hope and believe, is to liberate the world. Nor is this right confined to cases in which the whole people of an existing government may choose to exercise it. Any portion of such people that *can* may revolutionize, and make their own of so much of the territory as they inhabit. More than this, a *majority* of any portion of such people may revolutionize, putttng down a *minority*, intermingled with, or near about them, who may oppose their movements. Such minority was precisely the case of the Tories of our own Revolution. It is a quality of revolutions not to go by old lines, or old laws ; but to break up both, and make new ones.  As to the country now in question, we bought it of France in 1803, and sold it to Spain in 1819, according to the President's statement.  After this, all Mexico, including Texas, revolutionized against Spain ; and still later, Texas revolutionized against Mexico.  In my view, just so far as she carried her revolution, by obtaining the *actual*, willing or unwilling submission of the people, *so far* the country was hers, and no further.

Now, sir, for the purpose of obtaining the very best evidence as to whether Texas had actually carried her revolution to the place where the hostilities of the present war commenced, let the President answer the interrogatories I proposed as before mentioned, or some other similar ones.  Let him answer fully, fairly and honestly.

But if he *cannot* or *will* *not* do this—if, on any pretense he shall refuse or omit it—then I shall be fully convinced, of what I more than suspect already, that he is deeply conscious of being in the wrong; that he feels the blood of this war, like the blood of Abel, is crying to heaven against him; that he ordered General Taylor into the midst of a peaceful Mexican settlement, purposely to bring on war; that originally having some strong motive—what I will not stop now to give my opinion concerning—to involve the two countries in a war, and trusting to escape scrutiny by fixing the public gaze upon the exceeding brightness of military glory—that attractive rainbow that rises in showers of blood—that serpent's eye that charms to destroy—he plunged into it, and has swept *on* and *on*, till, disappointed in his calculation of the ease with which

Mexico might be subdued, he now finds himself he knows not where.

How can we obtain indemnity for the expenses of this war if those expenses amount to more than the whole value of the Mexican territory ?  Again, half the territory is already appropriated as private property ; how then are we to make anything out of these lands with this incumbrance on them, or how remove the incumbrance? I suppose no one will say we should kill the people, or drive them out, or make slaves of them, or even confiscate their property.          *          *          *          *          *          *

Again, it is a singular omission in this message, that it nowhere intimates *when* the President expects the war to terminate.  At its beginning, General Scott was, by this same President, driven into disfavor, if not disgrace, for intimating that peace could not be conquered in less than three or four months.  But now at the end of about twenty months, during which time our arms have given us the most splendid successes—every department, and every part, land and water, officers and privates, regulars and v lunteers, doing all that men could do, and hundreds of things which it had ever before been thought that men could *not* do ; after all this, this same President gives us a long message without showing us that, *as to the end*, he has himself even an imaginary conception.  As I have before said, he knows not where he is.  He is a bewildered, confounded, and miserably-perplexed man.  God grant he may be able to show that there is not something about his conscience more painful than all his mental perplexity.

On the 20th of June, 1848, he said : I wish now to sub-

mit a few remarks on the general proposition of amending
the Constitution. As a general rule, 1 think we would do
much better to let it alone. No slight occasion should
tempt us to touch it. Better not take the first step, which
may lead to a habit of altering it. Better rather habituate
ourselves to think of it as unalterable. It can scarcely
be made better than it is. New provisions would intro-
duce new difficulties, and thus create and increase appetite
for further change. No, sir; let it stand as it is. New
hands have never touched it. The men who made it have
done their work, and have passed away. Who shall im-
prove on what *they* did?

The first session of the Thirtieth Congress was prolonged
far beyond the date of the Presidential nominations of
1848, and the canvas was actively carried on by members
on the floor of the house. Mr. Lincoln warmly sustained
the nomination of Gen. Taylor, and before the adjourn-
ment of Congress, he made, in accordance with precedent
and general practice, one of his characteristic campaign
speeches. He showed himself a man of decided partisan
feelings, and entered into this contest with zeal, not only
repelling the violent attacks upon the Whig candidate, but
showing that there were blows to be given as well as
taken. He said some things in a vein of sarcastic humor,
which could only have been mistaken for actual bitterness,
by those who did not know the really genial character of
the man. Argument, ridicule and illustrative anecdotes
were brought into requisition, with great ability and un-
sparing boldness, in setting the real issues of the canvas,

political and personal, in what he deemed a proper light before the people.

We quote the following characteristic and interesting extracts from this speech :

### WHAT A PRESIDENT SHOULD BE.

My friend from Indiana has aptly asked, "Are you willing to trust the people?" Some of you answered, substantially, "We are willing to trust the people; but the President is as much the representative of the people as Congress." In a certain sense, and to a certain degree, he is the representative of the people. He is elected by them, as well as Congress is. But can he, in the nature of things, know the wants of the people as well as three hundred other men coming from all the various localities of the nation? If so, where is the propriety of having a Congress? That the Constitution gives the Preside t a negative on legislation, all know; but that this negative should be so combined with platforms and other appliances as to enable him, and, in fact, almost compel him, to take the whole legislation into his own hands, is what we object to—is what Taylor objects to—and is what constitutes the broad distinction between you and us. To thus transfer legislation is clearly to take it from those who understand with minuteness the interest of the people, and give it to one who does not and can not so well understand it.

### PLATFORMS.

One word more, and I shall have done with this branch of the subject. You Democrats, and your candidate, in the main, are in favor of laying down, in advance, a platform—a set of party positions, as a unit; and then of enforcing the people, by every sort of appliance, to ratify them, however unpalatable some of them may be. We, and our candidate, are in favor of making Presidential elections and the legislation of the country distinct matters; so that the people can elect whom they please, and afterward legislate just as they please, without any hindrance, save only so much as may guard against infractions of the Constitution, undue haste, and want of consideration. The difference between us is clear as noonday. That we are right we can not doubt. We hold the true Republican position. In leaving the people's business in their hands, we can not be wrong. We are willing, and even anxious, to go to the people on this issue.

### ONE OF HONEST ABE'S JOKES.

The other day, one of the gentlemen from Georgia (Mr. Iverson), an eloquent man, and a man of learning, so far as I can judge, not being learned myself, came down upon us astonishingly. He spoke in what the Baltimore *American* calls the "scathing and withering style." At the end of his second severe flash I was struck blind, and found myself feeling with my fingers for an assurance of my continued physical existence. A little of the bone was left, and I gradually revived. The gentleman gave us a second speech yesterday, all well considered and put down in writing, in which Van Buren was scathed and withered a "few' for his present position and movements. I can not remember the gentleman's precise language, but I do remember he put Van Buren down, down, till he got him where he has finally to "stink" and "rot."

## A TRACTABLE PRESIDENT.

In 1846 Cass was for the Wilmot Proviso, *at once;* in March, 1847 he was still for it, *but not just then;* in December, 1847, he was against it altogether. This is a true index to the whole man. When the question was raised in 1846, he was in a blustering hurry to take ground for it. He sought to be in the advance, not as a mere follower; but soon he began to see glimpses of the great Democratic ox-gad waving in his face, and to hear indistinctly a voice saying, "back, back, sir, back a little." He shakes his head and bats his eyes, and blunders back to his position of March, 1847; but still the gad waves, and the voice grows more distinct, and sharper still—" back, sir! back, I say! further back!" and back he goes to the position of December, 1847; at which the gad is still, and the voice soothingly says—" So! Stand still at that."

### WONDERFUL PHYSICAL CAPACITIES.

But I have introduced Gen. Cass's accounts here chiefly to show the wonderful physical capacities of the man. They show that he not only did the labor of several men at the same *time,* but that he often dit it at several *places,* many hundred miles apart, *at the same time.* And at eating, too, his capacities are shown to be quite as wonderful. From October, 1821, to May, 1822, he ate ten rations a day in Michigan, ten rations a day here, in Washington, and near five dollar's worth a day besides, partly on the road between the two places. And then there is an important discovery in his example—the art of being paid for what one eats, instead of having to pay for it. Hereafter, if any nice young man shall owe a bill which he can not pay in any other way, he can just board it out. Mr. Speaker, we have all heard of the animal standing in doubt between two stacks of hay, and starving to death; the like of which would never happen to Gen. Cass. Place stacks a thousand miles apart, he would stand stock still, midway between them, and eat them both at once; and the green grass along the line would be apt to suffer some too, at the same time. By all means, make him President, gentlemen. He will feed you bounteously—if—if there is any left after he shall have helped himself.

This speech exhibits the man in all the phrases of his character—acute, discerning, good humored, sarcastic, s n. ceer and industrious.

After the session closed, Mr. Lincoln made a visit to New England, where he delivered some effective campaign speeches, which were enthusiastically received by his large audience, as appears from the reports in the journals of those days, and as will be remembered by thousands. His time, however, was chiefly given, during the Congressional recess, to the canvass in the West, where, through the personal strength of Mr. Cass as a North-western man, the contest was more severe and exciting than in any other part of the country. The final triumph of Gen. Taylor, over all the odds against him, did much to counterbalance, in Mr. Lincoln's mind, the dishearting defeat of four years previous. He had declined to be a candidate for re-election to Congress, yet he had the satisfaction of aiding to secure, in his own district, a majority of 1,500 for the Whig Presidential candidates.

Mr. Lincoln again took his seat in the House in December, on the reasembling of the thirtieth Congress for its second session.

With the termination of the Thirtieth Congress, by Constitutional limitation, on the 4th of March, 1849, Mr. Lin.oln's career as a Congressman came to a close. He had refused to be a candedate for re-election in a district that had given him over 1,500 majority in 1846, and nearly the same to Gen. Taylor, as the Whig candidate for the Presidency in 1848. It does not appear that he desired or would have accepted any place at Washington, among the many at the disposal of the incoming Administration, in whose behalf he had so zealously labored. He retired once more to private life, renewing the professional practice which had been temporarily interrupted by his public employment. The duties of his responsible position had been discharged with assiduity and with fearless adherence to his convictions of right, under whatever circumstances. Scarcely a list of yeas and nays can be found, for either session, which does not contain his name. He was never conveniently absent on any critical vote. He never shrank from any responsibility which his sense of justice impelled him to take. His record, comparatively brief as it is, is no doubtful one, and will bear the closest scrutiny. And though one of the youngest and most inexperienced members of an uncommonly able and brilliant Congress, he would long have been remembered, without the mere recent events which have naturally followed upon his previous career, as standing among the first in rank of the distinguished statesmen of the Thirtieth Congress.

Returning to Springfield where he successfully continued his law practice, Mr. Lincoln did not take any part in public affairs until the introduction of the Kansas-Nebraska bill, in 1848. Roused to a sense of the danger which menaced the country, he at once took the field, and spoke against Douglas all over the State, with tremendous effect.

In 1856, he took active part in the formation of the Republican party, and sustained the nomination of Fremont and Dayton against Buchanan.

The main, the wild principles of the party are exhibited. in the following resolution of 1854 :

*Resolved*, That the doctrine affirmed by the Nebraska Bill, and gilded over by its advocat.s with the specious phrases of non-interventicn and popular sovereignty, is really and clearly a complete surrender of all the ground hitherto asserted and maintained by the Federal Govern-men·, with respect to the limitation of slavery, is a plain confession of the right of the slaveholder to transfer his human chattels to any part of the public domain, and there hold them as slaves as long as inclination or interest may dictate ; and that this is an attempt totally to reverse the doctrine hitherto uniformly held by statesmen and jurists, that slavery is the creature of local and State law, and to make it a national institution.

*Resolved*, That as freedom is national and slavery sectional and local, the absence of all law upon the subject of slavery presumes the existence of a state of freedom alone, while slavery exists only by virtue of positive law.

And by the following preamble and principal resolution of 1856 :

WHEREAS, The present Administration has prostituted

its powers, and devoted all its energies to the propagation
of slavery, and to its extension into Territories heretofore
dedicated to freedom, against the known wishes of the
people of such Territories, to the suppression of the freedom of speech, and of the press; and to the revival of
the odious doctrine of constructive treason, which has always been the resort of tyrants, and their most powerful
engine of injustice and oppression ; *and, whereas,* we are
convinced that an effort is making to subvert the principles, and ultimately to change the form of our Government, and which it becomes all ; atriots, all who love their
country, and the cause of human freedom, to resist; therefore,

*Resolved,* That we hold, in accordance with the opinions
and practices of all the great statesmen of all parties, for
the first sixty years of the administration of the Government, that, under the Constitution, Congress possesses
full power to prohibit slavery in the Territories ; and that
while we will maintain all Constitutional rights of the
South, we also hold that justice, humanity, the principles
of freedom as expressed in our declaration of Independence, and our National Constitution, and the purity and
perpetuity of our Government require that that power
should be everted, to prevent the extension of slavery into
Territories heretofore free.

Upon the accession of Mr. Buchanan to the presidential chair, the affairs of Kansas continued to be hotly dis-
cussed by both parties. Judge Douglas has again and
again been confronted by Mr. Lincoln, who, while taking
pains to show that he was neither an ama'gamationist or

an emancipationist, he heartily and honestly opposed that of the extension of slavery into the territories, but even the idea that slavery existed by any other right than the absence of express law to put it down. We quote:

"There is a natural disgust, in the minds of nearly all white people, to the idea of an indiscriminate amalgamation of the white and black races; and Judge Douglas evidently is basing his chief hope upon the chances of his being able to appropriate the benefit of this disgust to himself. If he can, by much drumming and repeating, fasten the odium of that idea upon his adversaries, he thinks he can struggle through the storm. He, therefore, clings to this hope, as a drowning man to the last plank. He makes an occasion for lugging it in from the opposition to the Dred Scott decision. He finds the Republicans insisting that the Declaration of Independence includes ALL men, black as well as white, and forthwith he boldly denies that it includes negroes all, and proceeds to argue gravely that all who counted it does, do so only because they want to vote, eat and sleep, and marry with negroes! He will have it that they cannot be consistent else. Now, I protest against the counterfeit logic which concludes that, because I do not want a black woman for a slave I must necessarily want her for a wife. I need not have her for either. I can just leave her alone. In some respects she certainly is not my equal; but in her natural right to eat the bread she earns with her own hands, without asking leave of any one else, she is my equal, and the equal of all others."

The campaign of 1858 was next ushered in. The Re-

publican party nominated Mr. Lincoln for U. S. Senator
in the place of Judge Douglas, whose term expired. It
was in the first speech which Mr. Lincoln made in this
memorable canvass that he used the immortal expression :
" I believe this government can not endure, permanently,
half slave and half free."

Judge Douglas answered in a spirited manner. He commenced : "I take great pleasure in saying that I have
known, personally and intimately, for about a quarter of
a century, the worthy gentleman who has been nominated
for my p'ace ; and I will say that I regard him as a kind,
amiable and intelligent gentleman, a good citiz n, and an
honorable opponent; and whatever issue I may have with
him will be of principle, and not involving personalities,"
and then went on : "Mr. Lincoln advocates boldly and
clearly a war of sections, a war of the North against the
South, of the free States against the slave States—a war
of extermination—to be continued relentlessly until the
one or the other should be subdued, and all the States
shall either become free or become slave."

But Mr. Lincoln triumphantly replied : "I did not say
that I was in favor of sectional war. I only said what I
expected would take place. I made a prediction only—it
may have been a foolish one perhaps. I did not even say
that I desired that slavery should be put in course of
ultimate extinction. I do say so now, however, so there
need be no longer any difficulty about that. It may be
written down in the next speech."

"I am not, in the first place, unaware that this Government has endured eighty-two years, half slave and half

free. I know that. I am tolerably well acquainted with the history of the country, and I know that it has endured eighty-two years, half slave and half free. I *believe*—and that is what I meant to allude to there—I *believe* it has endured, because during all that time, until the introduction of the Nebraska bill, the public mind did rest all the time in the belief that slavery was in course of ultimate extinction. That was what gave us the rest that we had through that period of eighty-two years; at least, so I believe. I have always hated slavery, I think, as much as any Abolitionist. I have been an Old Line Whig. I have alwyas hated it, but I have always been quiet about it until this new era of the introduction of the Nebraska Bill began."

Although Mr. Lincoln was not returned, yet the popular vote for senator was over four thousand majority his favor.

Admiration of the manly bearing and gallant conduct of Mr. Lincoln, throughout this campaign, which had early assumed a national importance, led to the spontaneous suggestion of his name, in various parts of the country, as a candidate for the Presidency. From the beginning to the end of the contest, he had proved himself an able statesman, an effective orator, a true gentleman, and an honest man. While, therefore, Douglas was returned to the Senate, there was a general presentiment that a juster verdict was yet to be had, and that Mr. Lincoln and his cause would be ultimately vindicated before the people. That time was to come, even sooner, perhaps, than his friends, in their momentary desponden-

cy, had expected. From that hour to the present, the
fame of Abraham Lincoln has been enlarging and ripen-
ing, and the love of his noble character has become more
and more deeply fixed in the popular heart.

During the following year he again gave himself up to
his profession ; but in the fall, when Douglas visited Ohio,
and endeavored to sway the Democracy of that State in
favor of the re-election of Mr. ·Pugh, Lincoln again took
the political field in opposition to him.

At Cincinnati on the 17th of September he said; allud-
ing to Douglas's perversions of his views, and to the
charge of wishing to disturb slavery in the States by
"shooting over" the line, Mr. Lincoln said :

### SHOOTING OVER THE LINE.

It has occured to me here to-night, that if I ever  do
shoot over at the people on the other side of the line in a
slave State, and purpose to do so, keeping my skin safe,
that I have now about the best chance I shall ever have.
[Laughter and applause.]  I should not wonder if there
are some Kentuckians about this audience ; we are close
to Kentucky ; and whether that be so or not, we are on
elevated ground, and by speaking distinctly, I should not
wonder if some of the Kentuckians should hear me on the
other side of the river.  [Laughter.]  For that reason I
propose to address a portion of what I have to say to the
Kentuckians.

I say, then, in the first place, to the Kentuckians, that I
am what they call, as I understand it, a "Black Rupubli-
can."  (Applause and Laughter.)  I think that slavery is
wrong, morally, socially and politically.  I desire that it

should be no further spread in these United States, and I
should not object if it should gradually terminate in the
whole Union. (Applause.) While I say this for myself,
I say to you, Kentuckians, that I understand that you
differ radically with me upon this proposition; that you
believe slavery is a good thing; that slavery is right; that
it ought to be extended and perpetuated in this Union.
Now, there being this broad difference between us, I do
not pretend in addressing myself to you, Kentuckians, to
attempt proselyting you at all; that would be a vain effort.
I do not enter upon it. I only propose to try to show you
that you ought to nominate for the next Presidency, at
Charleston, my distinguished friend, Judge Douglas
(Applause.)

### WHAT THE OPPOSITION MEAN TO DO.

I will tell you, so far as I am authorized to speak for
the Opposition, what we mean to do with you. We mean
to treat you, as nearly as we possibly can, as Washington,
Jefferson, and Madison treated you. (Cheers.) We mean
to leave you alone, and in no way to interfere with your
institutions; to abide by all and every compromise of the
Constitution; and, in a word, coming back to the original
proposition, to treat you, so far as degenerated men (if we
have degenerated) may, imitating the examples of those
noble fathers—Washington, Jefferson, and Madison. We
mean to remember that you are as good as we; that
there is no difference between us other than the difference
of circumstances. We mean to recognise and bear in
mind always that you have as good hearts in your bosom
as other people, or as we claim to have, and treat you

accordingly. We mean to marry your girls when we have a chance—the white ones I mean (Laughter) and I have the honor to inform you that I once got a chance that way myself ( A voice, "good for you," and Applause.)

In the spring of 1860, Mr. Lincoln yielded to the calls which came to him from the East for his presence and aid in the exciting political canvasses there going on. He spoke at various places in Connecticut, New Hampshire, and Rhode Island, and also in New York city, to very arge audiences, and was everywhere warmly welcomed. Perhaps one of the greatest speeches of his life, was that delivered by him at the Cooper Institute, in New York, on the 27th of February, 1860. A crowded audience was present, which received Mr. Lincoln with enthusiastic demonstrations. William Cullen Bryant presided, and introduced the speaker in terms of high compliment to the West, and to the " eminent citizen" of that section, whose political labors in 1856 and '58 were appropriately eulogised.

This is the last of the great speeches of Mr. Lincoln in this never to be forgotten canvas. It forms a brilliant close to this period of his life, and a fitting prelude to that on which he has next to enter.

It was during this visit to New York that the following incident occurred, as related by a teacher in the Five-Points House of Industry, in that city :

Our Sunday-school in the Five Points was assembled, one Sabbath morning, a few months since, when I noticed a tall, and remarkable-looking man enter the room and take a seat among us. He listened with fixed attention to

our exercises, and his countenance manifested such genuine interest, that I approached him and suggested that
he might be willing to say something to the children. He
accepted the invitation with evident pleasure, and coming
forward began a simple address, which at once facinated
every little hearer, and hushed the room into silence. His
language was strikingly beautiful, and his tones musical
with intense feeling. The little faces around would
droop into sad conviction as he uttered sentences of
warning, and would brighten into sunshine as he spoke
cheerful words of promise. Once or twice he attempted
to close his remarks, but the imperative shout of "Go on!"
"Oh, do go on!" would compel him to resume. As I
looked upon the gaunt and sinewy frame of the stranger,
and marked his powerful head and determined features,
now touched into softness by the impressions of the moment, I felt an irrepressible curiosity to learn something
more about him, and when he was quietly leaving the room,
begged to know his name. He courteously replied, "It is
Abra'm Lincoln, from Illinois!"

Upon the assembling of the Republican National Convention at Chicago, May 16, 1860, it soon became apparent
that the contest was to be narrowed down to two names—
those of Wm. H. Seward of New York, and Abraham
Lincoln of Illinois. On the first ballot Seward received
173, and Lincoln 102; on the second Seward received 184,
and Lincoln 181; on the third Lincoln received 231, and
Seward 180, Messrs. Chase, Cameron, Bates, Dayton, and
McLean receiving the balance, to make up the whole

number, or 464. This secured Mr. Lincoln the nomination.

The scene which followed—the wild manifestations of
approval and delight, within and without the hall, prolonged uninterruptedly for twenty minutes, and renewed
again and again for half an hour longer—no words can
describe. Never before was there a popular assembly of
any sort, probably, so stirred with a contagious and all-
pervading enthusiasm. The nomination was made unani-
mous, on motion of Mr. Everts, of New York, who had
presented the name of Mr. Seward, and speedily, on the
wings of lightning, the news of the great event was spread
to all parts of the land. Subsequently, with like heartiness
and unanimity the ticket was completed by the nomination, on the second ballot, of Senator Hannibal Hamlin, of
Maine, for Vice-President.

On the 23d, Mr. Lincoln addressed the following letter
of acceptance to the Convention :

SPRINGFIELD, ILL., May 23, 1860.

HON. GEO. ASHMUN,

*President of the Republican National Convention :*

SIR :—I accept the nomination tendered me by the convention over which you presided, and of which I am formally apprised in the letter of yourself and others, acting
as a committee of the convention for that purpose.

The declaration of principles and sentiments which accompanies your letter meets my approval; and it shall be
my care not to violate, nor disregard it, in any part.

Imploring the assistance of Divine Providence, and with
due regard to the views and feelings of all who were rep-

resented in the convention; to the rights of all the States, and Territories, and the people of the nation; to the inviolability of the Constitution, and to the perpetual union, harmony and prosperity of all, I am most happy to cooperate for the practical success of the principles declared by the convention.

Your obliged friend and fellow-citizen,

ABRAHAM LINCOLN.

We have thus followed this great statesman, this kind-hearted, genial man, this uncouth but warm-hearted Western pioneer, from his obscure home in the wilderness to his nomination to the highest office in the gift of the nation. We have now to speak of him after four years of varied experience in this office. We shall endeavor to do so without fear or favor.

---

## CHAPTER V.

### THE PRESIDENT.

*The hour. Mr. Lincoqn's relnctance to begin hostilities. The temper of the people and of Cougress. The battle of Bull Ruu. Preperations for a portable struggle. War meacsures. Mr. Lincoln not responsible for them. The slavery question. Mr. Lindoln's comprmi.e. Euancipation bill. The Emancipation Proclamation· Personal appearance and habits of the President. Finalcial measures. Determanation to restore the Union. The Confederate election. The end.*

In reviewing the career of President Lincoln during his past four years of office we must not only bear in mind what lets our previous opinions were, but as for public opinion and the acts of Congress have attended to influence its conduct.

Taking all these into proper consideration we have frequent occasions as we go along to admire the profound patriotism and practical wisdom and common sense which has distinguished his Presidential term.

First of all, was it or was it not wise in Mr. Lincoln to call for 75,000 troops on the 15th of April, 1861, and by this act accept the gage of battle which the bombardment of Fort Sumter had thereon drawn. It would scarcely be worth while to assume this question which the nation itself has answered so often, were there not left multitudes of our fellow citizens who still believe that Mr. Lincoln inaugurated this war, notwithstanding the most direct proofs to the contrary.

Now wherein was Mr. Lincoln to blame? He was duly elected President of the United States and took his oath of office at a junction where the stoutest mind might fairly have quailed from the task before it.

The Southern States seeing in his election the triumph of a party whose principles were objectionable to them, and forgetting that the limited power of a pres'dent must ever restrict him in time of peace from doing them any harm, had resolved to strike for their independence. Mr. Lincoln's duty was plain. The right of revolution he here denied, when he said in his speech of January 12, 1858, quoted on a previous page, "Any people may, when *having the power*, have the right." He had either to assume all the responsibilities of admitting the doctrine of peaceful secession, or open the door to a civil war that might not only last for many years, but lead in the end to military ascendency and the loss of our own liberties at home. It was a moment of eventful hesitation. During this period the news came of Sumter's fall, and the entire North was raised to a pitch of intense excitement. The people were lashed into fury, and men asked each other impatiently if Mr. Lincoln intended to submit to this thing any longer. It was with extreme reluctance that Honest Abe at last gave the signal. It was only when all other argume.ts had failed that the last of all arguments was employed, the argument of brute force, of war, war upon our brethren, maddened into fury by their own groundless apprehensions.

Mr. Lincoln felt as we all did at the time, that the war was a mere bagatelle, and would soon be over. The 75,000 troops were expected to awe the South into an attitude of reason, even without striking a blow. They were only called out for three months. Excited meetings held all over the North in support of the government, and denunciation of suspe.ted secessionists, gave the most posit've proof that the people were for strong measures. Had Mr. Lincoln acted in contradiction to this state of feeling, he would have been false to his office and his oath. It was not until the 4th of May that three years volunteers were called for. Meanwhile, the popular demonstrations for coercion were too unmistaken. Flags were raised, newspapers compelled to change their tone, public speakers called to order, and everything made to run in Union channels. On the 4th of July an extra sesssion of Congress was called, when the President recommended the raising of 400,000 men, and $400,000,000. The battles of Phillipi and Big Bethel had been fought; the war was inevitable. If Mr. Lincon had been the rankest of secessionists the war would have gone on just the same. The temper of Congress demonstrated this. Had he even chosen to veto the war measures it passed, they would have been passed again over his head. How then can the charge of inciting this war be held against Mr. Lincoln? The thing is untenable.

The events of the fortnight succeeding the meeting of Congress must be still fresh in every American mind. On the 21st of July the battle of Bull Run was fought. Here comes a pause in history. Both parties at once became aware that the struggle was to be one of life and death. It was to be no armed mob on one side, and a sheriff's *posse comitatus* on the other. Well-trained armies were to meet each other in strategic fields, and battle perhaps for many a year for union or dissolution. Still the majority of the people and with them the President and his cabinet believed that a few months preparation would fit our armies for the work of quick triumph. If Mr. Lincoln believed otherwise, if he foresaw that years might pass away before peace was restored, if he caught but a single glimpse of the " many possible phases into which civil war might grow," if he remembered that while we were making preparation the enemy was doing the same, he was guilty of a great wrong in not making the people better informed. Then, if they saw fit, they could either have gone on as they have done, or relinquished the Union at the start, and had done with it. But we have no reason to suppose that Mr. Lincoln saw farther than others did in these matters. Indeed, it was impossible to foresee, for both the temper of the South and its resources for war were hidden from us. And the temper of the North was to unequivocal to permit us to believe she would ever have consented to any other course than the one she adopted.

Says Mr. Alex. Delmar, the biographer of General McClellan : " Before the breaking out of the war, there were, in the first wild days of national excitement, but two parties—those for and those against the South—or, Secessionists and Unionists. No one stopped to think of the many possible phases into which civil war might grow. It was expected that it would end in a few days with an inevitable re-establishment of the national authority, and that consequently, any man who had proved so treacherous as to raise his voice in favor of the enemy, would ever afterward be pointed at as a traitor. So there were only two sides to the question—Union or Secession." *

This furnishes the key to the first part of Mr. Lincoln's administration. He had either to be for or against the South, either for Union or Secession. At this period the questions of expatiation, confiscation, amnesty, disposal of fugitive slaves, conscription, suppression of spoken and printed discontent at home, emancipation, national debt, occupation of conquered territory, &c., &c., had not been touched upon. But during that time, when the army of the Potomac under Mc Clellan was being organized for an earnest contest, these matters began to loom forth from amidst the terrible confusion of interests and revulsion of

* Life of Geo B. Mc Clellan, Published by T. R, DAWLEY, N. Y.

ideas, which are always occasioned by civil war. The *Democratic Standard*, of Concord, New Hampshire, was suppressed by soldiers and its office destroyed, the *War Bulletin*, and *Missourian* of St. Louis, suppressed by Gen. Fremont, the writ of *Habeas Corpus* served on Col. Burke at Fort Lafayette was refused to be obeyed, and the sum of $15,000 levied upon the people of St Joseph, Mis. by Gen. Pope. The *Jeffersonian*, at Westchester, Pa., was cleaned out, the *New York War Path, Daily News, Journal of Commerce*, and *Day Book* refused the privilege of the mails, the Philadelphia *Christian Observer* office closed by the U.'S. marshall, contrabands harbored at Fortress Monroe, secession meetings broken up at Stralenburg, N. J., and other points, martial law proclaimed all over Missouri, and Democratic, or Recognition newspapers indicted by·grand juries. Oaths of allegiance were introduced, that administered to Ross Winans, of Baltimore, in September 1861, being an instance; $33,000 in the St. Louis Savings Association were confiscated as being the property of the Cherokees who had joined the Confederates, amnesty offered by Gen. Wilson in Kentucky, contrabands supplied with food raiment and money by Gen. Wool, the writ of *Habeas Corpus* suspended by the President, military paroles and exchanges inaugerated, John C. Breckenridge indicted for treason, exportation of war materials prohibited, and a variety of other measures, none of which were dreamed of six months ago, were put in force. This state of affairs did not last long. New political ideas were broached every day; new phases of national existence disclosed themselves; new measures became necessary. Was it

strange that Mr, Lincoln should have differed a little from
the opinions he had previously applied to a state of peace
and inaction, or to a state of one just ushered in, and
bidding fair to end almost immediately.

The fall campaigns of 1861, and the spring campaign of
1862, next followed. During the former, we gained
Roanoke Island and the sea board of North Carolina, occupied Norfolk, captured the Forts on the Tennessee and
upper Mississippi, and gained various successes at other
points. During the latter, New Orleans was captured and
the celebrated Peninsular campaign inaugurated. This
campaign at once demonstrated the great power of our
enemies to carry on war—a power which before was seriously questioned.

It was now seen to be impossible to carry on the war,
and at the same time have that strict regard for the nor-
mal rights of those who stood with arms in their hands to
defy us, which had been promised when the war seemed
to be but a transient affair. Confiscation of rebel property
was deemed a matter of necessity, both as a just retalia-
tion for the rebel confiscation of Northern debts and
property, and as a war measure to weaken the resources
of the enemy.

The imprisonment of active secessionists was another
measure of necessity. To leave these persons to openly
preach and practice doctrines against which the majority
had declared and were fighting, was impossible. Even
in executing it, much forbearance was exhibited. To every
one imprisioned there were hundreds who escaped. Some
mistakes were made of course, but these could not be

helped, however much they were to be regretted. Once admit that the war was unavoidable, and we cannot well see how the contrary can be established, all the rest followed as the natural result of war.

On the 1st of December, 1862, the President, confident that without slavery the rebellion could never have existed; without slavery it could not continue, had embodied in his annual message to Congress a proposition of gradual emancipation. This proposition, which proved that he was still opposed to violent measures on this subject, was couched in the following terms :

"*Resolved by the Senate and House of Representatives of the United States of America in Congress assembled,* (two thirds of both Houses concurring) that the following articles be purposed to the Legislatures (or conventions) of the several States, as amendments to the Constitution of the United States, all or any of which articles when ratified by three fourths of the said Legislatures (or conventions) to be valid as part or parts of the said Constitution, namely:

"ARTICLE.—Every State wherein slavery now exists, which shall abolish the same therein, at any time, or times, before the first day of January, in the year of our Lord one thousand nine hundred, shall receive compensation from the United States, to wit :

"The President of the United States shall deliver to every such State bonds of the United States, bearing interest at the rate of — per cent. per annum, to an amount equal to the aggregate sum of ———— for each slave shown to have been therein, by the eighth census of the United

States, said bonds to be delivered to such States by installments, or in one parcel at the completion of the abolishment, accordingly as the same shall have been gradual, or at one time, within such State; and interest shall begin to run upon any such bond only from the proper time of its delivery aforesaid. Any State having received bonds as aforesaid, and afterwards re-introducing or tolerating slavery therein, shall refund to the United States the bonds so received or the value thereof, and all interest paid thereon.

"ARTICLE.—All slaves who shall have enjoyed actual freedom by the chances of the war at any time before the end of the rebellion, shall be forever free; but all owners of such, who shall not have been disloyal, shall be compensated for them, at the same rates as is provided for States adopting abolishment of slavery, but in such way that no slave shall be twice accounted for.

"ARTICLE.—Congress may appropriate money and otherwise provide for colonizing free colored persons, with their own consent, at any place or places without the United States."

This proposition contained two measures, one of gradual emancipation with compensation, and the other recognizing the freedom of those who had already gained it of their own effort.

Though the former was never adopted by the States, the latter was afterwards developed into the celebrated emancipation proclamation of January 1, 1863.

The President's mind was gradually changing. At first he was for avoiding all interference with slavery, except so far as regarded the District of Columbia. But the war by disclosing the irreconcilable interests of free and slave labor taught him that the Union must, to remain inviolate, become either all free or all slave. Besides that, slavery was discovered to be a source of strength instead of an element of weakness to the rebels so long as we respected it, and it became necessary to the success of the war that a blow should be levelled at it. Reluctant to the last to inaugurate such a policy, Mr. Lincoln offered this bill as a compromise. He accompanied it with these words :

"Among the friends of Union there is great diversity of sentiment and of policy, in regard to slavery and the African race among us. Some would perpetuate slavery; some would abolish it suddenly and without compensation; some would abolish it gradually and with compensation; some would remove the freed people from us, and some would retain them with us; and there are yet other minor diversities. Because of these diversities, we waste much strength in struggles among ourselves. By mutual concession we should harmonize and act together. This would be compromise; but it would be compromise among the friends, and not with the enemies of the Union. These articles are not intended to embody a plan of such mutual concessions. If the plan shall be adopted, it is assumed that emancipation will follow, at least in several of the States."

But it was too late. The Southerners would not back down, clearly in the wrong as they were, and the war went on.

During this time Mr. Lincoln worked night and day in his office.

The routine of his daily life we can give in no better words than those in which it is related in the volume of Old Abe's Jokes, published by T. R. Dawley :

"Mr. Lincoln is an early riser, and he thus is able to de-vote two or three hours each morning to his voluminous private correspondence, besides glancing at a city paper. At nine he breakfasts—then walks over to the war office, to read such war telegrams as they give him, (occasionlly some are withheld,) and to have a chat with General Hal-leck on the military situation, in which he takes a great interest. Returning to the White House, he goes through with his morning's mail, in company with a private secre-tary, who makes a minute of the reply which he is to make —and others the President retains, that he may answer them himself. Every letter receives attention, and all which are entitled to a reply receive one no matter how they are worded, or how inelegant the chirography may be.

"Tuesdays and Fridays are cabinet days, but on other days visitors at the White House are requested to wait in the anti-chamber, and send in their cards. Sometimes, before the President has finished reading his mail Louis will have a handful of pasteboard, and from the cards laid before him Mr. Lincoln has visitors ushered in, giving pre-cedence to acquaintances. Three or four hours do they pour in, in rapid succession, nine out of ten asking offices, and patiently does the President listen to their application. Care and anxiety have furrowed his rather homely features yet occasionally he is 'reminded of an anecdote' and good humored glances beam from his clear, grey eyes, while his ringing laugh shows that he is not 'used up' yet, The simple and natural manner in which he delivers his thoughts makes him appear to those visiting him like an earnest, affectionate friend. He makes little parade of his legal science, and rarely indulges in speculative propositions, but states his ideas in plain Anglo-Saxon, illumina ted by many lively images and pleasing allusions, which seem to flow as if in obedience to a restless impulse of nature. Some newspaper admirer attempts to deny that the President tells stories. Why, it is rarely that any one is in his company for five minutes without hearing a good tale, appropriate to the subject talked about. Many a metaphysical argument does he demolish by simply telling an anecdote, which exactly overturns the verbal structure.

About four o'clock the President declines seeing any more company, and often accompanies his wife in her carriage to take a drive. He is fond of horseback exercise, and when passing the summers home, used generally to go in the saddle. The President dines at six, and it is rare that some personal friends do not grace the round dining table where he throws off the cares of office, and reminds those who have been in Kentucky of the old school gentleman who used to dispense generous hospitality there.—From the dinner table the party retire to the crimson drawing room, where coffee is served, and where the President passes the evening, unless some dignitary has a special interview. Such is the almost unvarying life of Abraham Lincoln, whose administration will rank next in importance to that of Washington in our national annals.

His portrait is thus drawn by an English writer:

"To say that he is ugly, is nothing; to add that his figure is grotesque, is to convey no adequate impression— Fancy a man over six feet high, and then out of proportion; with long bony arms and legs, which somehow seem to be always in the way, with great, rugged, furrowed hands, which grasp you like a vice when shaking yours; with a long snaggy neck, and a chest too narrow for the great arms at its side. Add to this figure a head cocoa-nut shaped and somewhat too small for such a stature, covered with rough, uncombed' and uncomable hair, that stands out in every direction at once; a face furrowed, wrinkled and indented, as though it had been scarred by vitrol; a high narrow forehead, and sunk deep beneath bushy eyebrows, two bright, dreamy eyes, that seem to gaze through you without looking at you; a few irregular blotches of black, bristly hair, in the place where beard and whiskers ought to grow; a close-set, thin-lipped, stern mouth, with two rows of large white teeth, and a nose and ears which have been taken by mistake from a head twice the size.—Clothe this figure, then, in a long, tight, badly-fitting suit of black, creased, soiled and puckered up at every salient point of the figure (and every point of this figure is salient) put on large, ill-fitting boots, gloves too long for the long, bony fingers, and a puffy hat, covered to the top with dusty, puffy crape; and then add to this an air of strength, physical as well as moral, and a strange look of dignity coupled with all this grotesqueness, and you will have the impression left upon me by Abraham Lincoln."

Many curious anecdotes are told of him and many by him, but as these would evidently be out of place in this volume we refer the reader to the work just quoted, where a very complete selection may be found.

In connection with Mr. Lincoln's administration it may not be out of place to make a few remarks with regard to the financial measures adopted by Congress, and approved by himself.

At the beginning of the war, the public debt was but eighty millions. The sum of four hundred millions was deemed necessary to purchase supplies, and organize our forces. This sum could not be raised in either money or goods, without fatal delay. The only two measures left were, either to raise it in small sums repeatedly, or at once by means of a paper issue. The first method would have been the better, but it required time, and in the end might not have succeeded. The second could be carried into effect immediately, and with absolute certainty of success. It presented but one disadvantage—that of legal tender. Without this quality, its success was at best very equivocal; with it, the organization and arming our forces could go on without accident or delay. Fully aware of its dangerous character, but assured that no other way was open to it, Congress passed the law of legal tender, and Mr. Lincoln approved it. Since that time, and up to the present, (October, 1864), various treasury bills have been passed by Congress, all based upon the legal tender act. The debt has increased to the sum of two thousand millions, of which seven hundred millions are legal tender currency, and the remainder short and long bonds, at various rates of interest and for various periods. This seven hundred millions of currency which, with the State bank's issues of one hundred and fifty millions, makes up three times as much currency, (foreign debts and domestic credits neutralizing each other), as the country requires for the purposes of trade. It is this which has caused the prices of gold and all other products of labor to be three times as much as of old. The debt of the country might be twice as much as it is, and if the total currency were not over three hundred millions, (commercial credits, &c., being equal), prices would recede to their former figures before the war. For this reason, it has ever been Mr. Lincoln's endeavor to curtail the circulation, and in his various messages he has always adhered to this desire. On the 19th of January, 1863, in a special message to Congress he took occasion, while approving of the one hundred million bill it had passed, to deprecate the farther issue of United States notes, as tending to inflate and debase the currency.

But his finalcial minister, Mr. Chase, did not prove equal to the emergency. He was accordingly removed on the 1st of July, 1864. Mr. Chase could not manage to raise money without increasing the currency. He was to much bound up in his pet system of National banks. Since then, Mr. Fessenden has demonstrated the thing to be practicable, and no furthur issues of any moment had been made. The debt has increased, bu. not the currency.

And now as regards the debt.  It has been a  continual
source of attack by those inimical to Mr.  Lincoln's administration, that the debt is almost equal to the entire wealth
of the loyal States.  This surplus wealth according to the
last census, amounted to about 3,000 millions of moveable
property, and 7,000 millions of real estate.

The latter, of course, being entirely useless as a basis of
credit or a means of supporting hostilities, we leave out
of the question.  The sum of 3,000 millions therefore truly
represented, we will say, the moveable or disposable
wealth of the loyal States in 1860.

Assuming that it has increased to 4,000 millions in tho
meantime, an increase very much below the usual rate
of augmentation, let us see how much of this has been
used up in the war.

The present debt is 7,000 millions, it is true, but it must
be remembered though this *does not represent over half its
amount of supplies.*  The balance represents profits, and
these profits are returned to the nation.  In other words
the rabid and reckless contractors and sutlers, have not
failed to charge double prices for every thing furnished to
the Government or soldiers, so that 7,000 millions of debt
only represent 1,000 millions of property consumed in the
war.  These unconscionable practices no longer exists, for
the Government is now wide awake , and cannot be
cheated so easily as it was with the Cataline, and the $3
condemned muskets, and other runious contracts made at
the outset of the war.

Contractors and sutlers now-a-days can do little more

than make an honest living. The days of public rapine
are gone by.

Thus we perceive that, with a debt that represents but
1,000 millions of actual property, out of 4,000 millions of
actual wealth, to say nothing of our lands and the bu'ld-
ings and other improvements thereon, the people of the
loyal United States have suffered but little in the aggregate, even from four years of gigantic warfare.

This fact alone should shed lustre upon the head of Mr.
Lincoln, who by his own strick regard for law and his ad-
miral measures of Administration, has kept the nation
intact, and enabled it to persue, even in the midst of war,
those peaceful arts, which alone can furnish means to
mantain a protracted struggle in the field.

Among the many admirable qualities of Mr. Lincoln,
there is none so noticeable as the warmth and purity of
style which characterizes his correspondence and official
documents. This is at once an index to the man's nature;
a nature lofty, simple, and ardent. What could be more
truly sublime than the sentiments addressed by Mr. Lincoln to the workingmen of Manchester, in response to a
letter from them approving of his manly and patriotic
course of action in the government of this country during
the two years and a half of civil war? What more simple
and unaffected than the charming note he addressed to Mr.
Hackett, the actor? What more ardent than the impas-
sioned appeal he addressed to the country upon the subject of the gradual Emancipation bill already quoted. Said
A. Lincoln in this memorable document :

" I do not forget the gravity which should characterize

a paper addressed to the Congress of the nation, by the Chief Magistrate of the nation. Nor do I forget that some of you are my seniors, nor that many of you have more experience than I, in the conduct of public affairs. Yet, I trust that in view of the great responsibility resting upon me, you will perceive no want of respect to yourselves, in any undue earnestness I may seem to display."

"Is it doubted, then, that the plan I propose, if adopted, would shorten the war, and thus lessen its expenditure of money and of blood? Is it doubted that it would restore the national authority and national prosperity, and perpetuate both indefinitely? Is it doubted that we here—Congress and Executive—can secure its adoption? Will not the good people respond to a united and earnest appeal from us? Can we, can they, by any other means, so certainly or so speedily, assure these vital objects? We can succeed only by concert. It is not 'can *any* of us *imagine* better,' but 'can we *all* do better?'

"The dogmas of the quiet past are inadequate to the stormy present. The occasion is piled high with difficulty, and we must rise with the occasion. As our case is new, so we must think anew, and act anew. We must disenthrall ourselves, and then we shall save our country.

"Fellow-citizens, we cannot escape history. We, of this Congress and this administration, will be remembered in spite of ourselves. No personal significance, or insignificance, can spare one or another of us. The fiery trial through which we pass will light us down in honor or dishonor, to the latest generation. We *say* we are for the Union. The world will not forget that we say this. We know how to save the Union. The world knows we do know how to save it. We—even *we* here—hold the power, and bear the responsibility. In *giving* freedom to the *slave* we *assure* freedom to the *free*—honorable alike in that we give and what we preserve. We shall nobly save, or meanly lose, the last best hope of earth. Other means may succeed; this could not fail. The way is plain, peaceful, generous, just—a way which, if followed, the world will forever applaud, and God must forever bless."

The writer is no hero-worshipper, and has refrained during the course of this work from rendering many a just tribute to Mr. Lincoln's character, for fear of falling into a style of adulation, but he appeals to any right-minded man, whatever be his political opinions, to say whether the foregoing extract is not full of beauties which necessarily reflect the mind that conceived it.

The italics are copied from the original, or we should have wished to italicise these lines.

" *Above al, fellow citizens, we cannot escape history, We of this Congress, and this Administration, will be remembered in spite of ourselves.*" What sincerity and truthfulness of mind shines all through these sentences! " *The fiery trial through which we pass will light us down in honor or dishonor to the latest generation.*' Can the lips which uttered these words be those of an *obscene* joker, the character with which he is charged by his political enemies?

" *We say we are for the Union. The world will not forget that we say this.*" Can the mind which prompted these noble words be the same, which, as these same enemies charge, longed for a ribald song over the heroic cerements of Gettysburg ? Impossible. The stately march of such a phrase as this never issued from a brain capable of low desires or impure thoughts. " *In giving freedom to the slave, or assure freedom to the free—honorble alike in what we give, and what we preserve.*" Mr. Lincoln is unquestionably of an affable temper and cheerful turn of mind ; he has an encouraging smile for this one, a joke for that, and a kind word for all. But he is never obscene in his seasonable merriment, and those who ascribe to him such a quality seriously mistake his character.

What can be more becoming, more respectful, more decorous, than this paragraph ?

" *I do not forget the gravity which should characterize a paper addressed to the Congress of the nation by the Chief Magistrate of the nation. Nor do I forget that some of you are my seniors ; nor that many of you have more experience than I, in the conduct of public affairs.* "

How like, it sounds, to the dignified address of Othello to the Venetian Senate, commencing : " Most potent, grave, and reverend segniors.

Be assured, fellow citizens, the man who can employ such language as this, upon occasions so eventful, is worthy of any distinction to which you can elevate him. Whatever the homeliness of his exterior, depend upon it, that honesty and true worth dwells beneath all.

In former days of European tumult the posessors of those masterpieces of art, each of which was a princely fortune of itself, resorted to a curious artifice to preserve their treasures from the sack and pillage of conquering armies. They covered over their pictures with a composition upon

which a second picture could be painted. This second or
outer picture was purposely executed as rudely as possible in order that its humble and unattractive appearance
might save it from being a deniable object to the marau-
ders.

In this manner a vast number of priceless masterpeices
escape destruction, although at the total cost of their merit,
until some appreciative hand of modern days detects the
false daub, and patiently removes it to disclose the match-
less future beneath.

It is such a task as this which we would delight to per-
form for the character of Mr. Lincoln—but our space for-
bids it, nor is it scarcely necessary in his case. The entire
nation has long since discovered what merits he possesses
millions of human eyes gazing upon him at once, how
pierce his faults and disclose his motives, and the verdict
of the people is, taking him for all in all, we call him
"Honest Abe."

We now approach those events of Mr. Lincoln's life,
which bear more pointedly upon the issues of the present
political campaign, and shall endeavor to dispose of them
as fairly and lightly as possible.

Upon his accession to power there were, as we have
said, but two political parties—that for, and that against
the South.

After the battle of Bull Run, and particularly after the
Peninsular campaign, there began to be a greater diversity of opinion on national subjects. It was felt that the
war was not to be a short one, and many honest citizens
began to inquire if it were not possible to pay too great a

price for Union. This produced the peace party, who differed from the Copperheads, or Secessionists, in this, that while they were in favor of letting the South go, they were so, not because they thought she has right, but because they feared that she would ultimately succeed, and all our energies have been needlessly wasted in attempting to prevent her. Besides that, they looked with alarm upon encroachments the government was obliged to make upon some of the reserved rights of the States, as in the case of a national currency, a conscription law, &c. They also apprehended nothing short of a declared despotism, from the cases of military and political arrests, &c., which now and then unavoidably occurred, and desired to put a stop to it at once.

The arrest of the Maryland Legislature and the incarceration of some irrepressible secessionists made them liken Mr. Lincoln to Oliver Cromwell. Democracy began to tremble for its existence. But they mistook the man, that's all. The fire of liberty truly is eternal vigilance, but the country might go to sleep and safely leave Abraham Lincoln to take a generous and jealous care of its liberties.

Then another party began to spring up. There were a number of jealous emancipationist who forgot that a nation is a cumbrous body and necessarily moves slowly, who were dissatisfied with Mr. Lincoln's slow and careful steps towards the settlement of the great question of negro slavery in the United States. They foresaw that in order to terminate the war, slavery must be forever exterminated, but they forgot that they were still but a minority, and that to but a remedy in force, which was opposed to the wishes of the majority, we only cause the evil to be the more adhered to. Time was required, as well as some more actual experience, to convince the nation that Union was impossible under the old terms. This necessary time the Radicals were for jumping over. To this Mr. Lincoln objected. They accordingly began to hate him with undisguised cordiality. They denounced him in Congress, and attacked him in a partisan press which they established, at the head of which was the *New Nation*, published by Gen. Fremont in New York, From the pulpit he was anathematized by such eminent political divines as the Rev. Dr. Cheever, while the rostrum poured forth bold denunciations through the speeches of Wendell Phillips. All Radicaldom was in arms against him. At the same time he was exposed to the attacks of the peace party or the Democracy, and had his hands full with the war, the government, and the copperheads, or secessionists.

But all these assaults proved futile. Mr. Lincoln was not to be swayed, either by book or bell. He kept on the even tenor of his way, with but one object in view—Union—all else being subservient to this one great idea.

When the time came to nominate a successor to the office he had filled with so much ability and integrity for over three years, Mr. Lincoln was again almost unanimously chosen by the convention, this time assembled at Baltimore. The vote for President in the Baltimore nominating convention, June 9, 1864, was as follows :

For Mr. Lincoln.—Maine 14, New Hampshire 10, Vermont 10, Massachusetts 24, Rhode Island 8, Connecticut

12, New York 66, New Jersey 14, Pennsylvania 52, Dela·
ware 6, Maryland 14, Louisiana 14, Arkansas 10, Tennessee 15, Kentucky 22, Ohio 42, Indiana 26, Illinois 32, Mich·
igan 16, Wisconsin 16, Iowa 16, Minnesota 8, California 10,
Oregon 6, West Virginia 10, Kansas 6, Nebraska 6, Colo-
rado 6, Nevada 6. Total 497.

For Gen. Grant.—Missouri 22.

The following are the resolutions constituting the platform :

*Resolved*, That it is the highest duty of every American
citizen to maintain against all their enemies the integrity
of the Union and the paramount authority of the Constitution and laws of the United States, and that, laying
aside all differences and political opinions, we pledge ourselves as Union men, animated by a common sentiment
and aiming at a common object, to do everything in our
power to aid the government in quelling by force of arms
the rebellion now raging against its authority, and in
bringing to the punishment due to their crimes the rebels
and traitors arrayed against it.

*Resolved*, That we approve the determination of the gov·
ernment of the United States not to compromise with
rebels or to offer any terms of peace, except such as may
be based upon an "unconditional surrender" of their hos·
tility and a return to their just allegiance to the Constitution and laws of the United States; and that we call
upon the government to maintain this position, and to
prosecute the war with the utmost possible vigor to the
complete suppression of the rebellion, in full reliance upon
the self-sacrifices, the patriotism, the heroic valor and the

undying devotion of the American people to their country and its free institutions.

*Resolved*, That as slavery was the cause and now constitutes the strength of this rebellion, and as it must be always and everywhere hostile to the principles of Republican government, justice and national safety demand its utter and complete extirpation from the soil of the republic, and that we uphold and maintain the acts and proclamations by which the government, in its own defence, has aimed a death blow at this gigantic evil; we are in favor, furthermore, of such an amendment to the Constitution, to be made by the people, in conformity with its provisions, as shall terminate and for ever prohibit the existence of slavery within the limits or the jurisdiction of the United States.

*Resolved*, That the thanks of the American people are due to the soldiers and sailors of the army and navy (applause), who have periled their lives in defense of their country and in vindication of the honor of the flag; that the nation owes to them some permanent recognition of their patriotism and their valor, and ample and permanent provisions for those of their survivors who have received disabling and honorable wounds in the service of the country; and that the memories of those who have fallen in its defense shall be held in grateful and everlasting remembrance.

*Resolved*, That we approve and applaud the practical wisdom, the unselfish patriotism, and unswerving fidelity to the Constitution and the principles of American liberty which Abraham Lincoln has discharged, under circumstances of unparalleled difficulty, the great duties and responsibilities of the Presidential office ; that we approve and indorse, as demanded by the emergency and essential to the preservation of the nation, and as within the Constitution, the measures and acts which he has adopted to defend the nation against its open and secret foes ; that we approve especially the proclamation of emancipation, and the employment as Union soldiers of men heretofore held in slavery, and that we have full confidence in his determination to carry these and all other constitutional measures essential to the salvation of the country into full and complete effect.

*Resolved*, That we deem it essential to the general welfare that harmony should prevail in the national councils and we regard as worthy of public confidence and official trust these only who cordially indorse the principles proclaimed in these resolutions, and which should characterize the administration of the government.

*Resolved*, That the government owes to all men employed in its armies, without regard to distinction of color, the full protection of the laws of war, and that any violation of these laws or of the usuages of civilized nations in the time of war by the rebels now in arms should be made the subject of full and prompt redress.

*Resolved*, That the foreign immigration which in the past has added so much to the wealth and development of resources and increase of power to this nation, the asylum of the oppressed of all nations, should be fostered and encouraged by a liberal and just policy.

*Resolved,* That we are in favor of the speedy construc‑ tion of the railroad to the Pacific.

*Resolved,* That the national faith pledged for the redemp‑ tion of the public debt, must be kept inviolate, and that for this purpose we recommend economy and rigid responsi‑ bility in the public expenditures, and a vigorous and just system of taxation ; that it is the duty of every loyal state to sustain the credit and promote the use of the national currency.

*Resolved,* That we approve the position taken by the government that the people of the United States can never regard with indifference the attempt of any European power to overthrow by force or to supplant by fraud the institutions of any republican government on the Western Continent, and that they will view with extreme jealousy as menacing to the peace and independence of this our country, the efforts of any such power to obtain new foot‑ holds for monarchial governments sustained by a foreign military force in near proximity to the United States.

Upon the news of his nomination being presented to Mr. Lincoln on the following day he made this charac teristic acceptance :

GENTLEMEN : I can only say in response to the remarks of your chairman, I suppose, that I am very grateful for the renewed confidence which has been accorded to me, both by the convention and by the National League. I am not insensible at all to the personal compliment there is in this, yet I do not allow myself to believe that any but a small portion of it is to be appropriated as a personal compliment. The convention and the nation, I am assured, are alike animated by a higher view of the interests of the country for the present and the great future, and that part I am entitled to appropriate as a compliment, is only that part which I may lay hold of as being the opinion of the convention and of the league—that I am not unworthy to be intrusted with the place I have occupied for the last three years. I have not permitted myself, gentlemen, to conclude that I am the best man in the country; but I am reminded in this connec ion of a story of an old Dutch farmer, who remarked to a companion once, that "it was not best to swap horses when crossing streams."

The laughter and applause which followed these remarks told the President he had not judged amiss of the cheerful confiding mood in which the momination had been made by the Convention. Gov. Andrew Johnson, of Tennessee, has associated with him in the ticket as candidate for Vice-President.

But the Radicals had nominated Gen. Fremont, and were determined to carry him. It was only when Mr. Lincoln, in order to place himself above the ordinary ambiguity of party platforms, issued his message "To whom it may Concern," that the Radicals at once forsook the leader they had chosen, and ranged themselves under the banner of "Lincoln, Union, and Liberty!" His message declared that Union was impossible without slavery was exterminated. The time had come. Mr. Lincoln followed it with reluctance, fearing that public opinion was not yet ripe. But he is not a day too soon. Even the Democracy have declared for Union. The question, therefore, is, whether we shall have a Union free from a system which has continually, and still threatens its existence, or one which shall be open to the same sad experiences we have already undergone. If the South knew its own interest, knew how much it has lost by its refusal to employ machinery and to manufacture cottons on the same spot where the staple was cultivated, it would come in at once and end the war. If the North knew that with the preservation of slavery, even with changed owners, the latter would soon become pro-slavery men, and renew the conflict of systems and interests over again, it would become anti-slavery at once, and join with us in elevating to the chief-magistracy the only man who has shown himself to be equal to the crisis—Abraham Lincoln, of Illinois. Let the event speak for itself.

There are now but two parties—those for the Union as it was, and those for the Union as it should be.

Let the choice be made.

Before bringing this biography to a close, it may not be uninteresting to give an account of the famous Bogus Proclamation of President Lincoln, the secret history of which has never before been published.

On the 14th of May last, the *Metropolitan Record*, of New York, published a bogus proclamation of Jefferson Davis to the people of the North, of which the following is a copy :

PROCLAMATION OF JEFFERSON DAVIS TO THE PEOPLE OF THE UNITED STATES.

[We shall not vouch for the authenticity of the following proclamation, particularly at a time when dubious documents considered reliable are given almost daily to

the public by the Secretary of the War Department.—ED.
METROPOLITAN RECORD.

It is now three years since it was announced, that sixty
days would be sufficient to compel the Southern States to
return to that Union, from which they had deliberately
severed all connection. It is needless to enter into ,a
review or consideration of the causes that led to this step
on their part. They are already familiar to the world.
We base our claim to self-government within the limits of
an independent Confederacy, on the principles of the
Revolution of Seventy-six, which established the Sovereignty of the State, as well as the freedom of the people.

My object in addressing you at the present time, is to
stay, if possible, the further effusion of blood. You must
be convinced at the end of three years strife, that the subjugation of the South is an impossibility, and that a
further prolongation of the war is a criminal expenditure
of life and treasure.

Upon your decision the question of peace or war now
rests. The independence of the South is a matter of
history, and its people have established in the eyes of the
world their claim to a separate national existence.

The Southern Confederacy has been called into being by
the will of the Southern people, and he who now addresses
you is their freely chosen President, elected, not by a
minority, but by a majority of their votes. In thus ex-
pressing his desire for peace he is but acting in accordance
with the dictates of humanity. Enough blood has been
shed to satisfy even the most sanguinary, and in proposing
a suspension of hostilities, an armistice, I am but com-

plying with the wishes of a portion of our people as expressed in the act of the Legislature of Georgia for the establishment of peace on what it is to be hoped will prove a satisfactory and permanent basis.

Shall this war be stopped or shall it continue? Upon your answer depends the issue.

This was doubtless intended by the editor as a bit of that Irish humor for which he is noted. It excited no attention. In a parrallel column giving an account of military affairs at the time when Grant was battling at Spottsylvania Court-house, occur these words:

WEDNESDAY NIGHT.
We cannot resist the conviction that the Army of the Potomac has met with disaster. The extravagant heading in large type with which the daily papers abound of " VICTORY !" " GLORIOUS SUCCESS !" " TOTAL DEFEAT OF LEE !" do not weigh with us. We have carefully sifted the immense mass of tangled and contradictory dispatches which have thus far come to hand, and we deliberately arrive at the conclusion, that until a totally different account shall have been placed before the public, *General Grant has been defeated.*

It will be seen that these two extracts contain the germs of that, which Joseph Howard a few days afterwards elaborated into a bogus proclamation of Mr. Lincoln.

The paper containing them was handed to Howard, who upon looking them over *asked what might be the effect* if Mr. Lincoln in a message to the people acknowledged Grant's defeats, and appointed *a day of public fasting and prayer.* He was assured that it would cause a universal feeling of depression at the North, and of course would effect the stock and gold markets.

The three days afterwards, the following document

appeared in the New York *World and Journal of Commerce :*

EXECUTIVE MANSION, May 17, 1864.

*Fellow-Citizens of the United States :*

In all seasons of exigency, it becomes a nation carefully to scrutinize its line of conduct, humbly to approach the Throne of Grace, and meekly to implore forgiveness, wisdom, and guidance.

For reasons known only to Him it has been decreed that this country should be the scene of unparalleled outrage, and this nation the monumental sufferer of the nineteenth century. With a heavy heart, but an undimnished confidence in our cause, I approach the performance of a duty rendered imperative by my sense of weakness before the Almighty and of justice to the people.

It is not necessary that I should tell you that the first Virginia campaign under Lt. Gen. Grant, in whom I have every confidence, and whose courage and fidelity the people do well to honor, is virtually closed. He has conducted his great enterprise with discreet ability. He has inflicted great loss upon the enemy. He has crippled their strength, and defeated their plans.

In view, however, of the situation in Virginia, the disaster at Red River, the delay at Charleston, and the general state of the country, I, Abraham Lincoln, do hereby recommend that Thursday, the 26th day of May, A. D., 1864, be solemnly set apart throughout these United States, as a day of fasting, humiliation and prayer.

Deeming, furthermore, that the present condition of public affairs presents an extraordinary occasion, and in view of the pending expiration of the service of (100,000) one hundred thousand of our troops, I, Abraham Lincoln, President of the United States, by virtue of the power vested in me by the Constitution and the laws, have thought fit to call forth, and hereby do call forth, the citizens of the United States between the ages of (18) eighteen and (45) forty-five years, to the aggregate number of (400,000) four hundred thousand, in order to suppress the existing rebellious combinations, and to cause the due execution of the laws.

And furthermore, in case any State or number of States shall fail to furnish by the fifteenth day of June next, their assigned quota, it is hereby ordered that the same be raised by an immediate and peremptory draft.

The details for this object will be communicated to the State authorities through the War Department.

I appeal to all loyal citizens to favor, facilitate, and aid this effort to mantain the honor, the integrity, and the existence of our National Union, and the perpetuity of popular government.

In witness whereof, I have hereunto set my hand, and caused the seal of the United States to be affixed.

Done at the City of Washington, this Seventeenth day of May, in the year of our Lord, one thousand eight hundred and sixty-four, and of the Independence of the United States, the eighty-eight. (Signed,) ABRAHAM LINCOLN.

By the President.

WILLIAM II. SEWARD, Secretary of State.

This production was at once stigmatized as a forgery, but not before it had caused a serious decline in gold and stocks, by which, it is presumed, Howard made large profits.

The Secretary of State, upon being informed of its appearance in the *World* and *Journal of Commerce*, addressed the following despatch to the Associated Press :

DEPARTMENT OF STATE, }
WASHINGTON, May 18th, 1864. }

TO THE PUBLIC.

A paper purporting to be a proclamation of the President, countersigned by the Secretary of State, and bearing date the 17th day of May, is reported to this Department as having appeared in the New York *World* of this date. This paper is an absolute forgery. No proclamation of this kind, or any other, has been made, or proposed to be made, by the President, or issued, or proposed to be issued by the State Department, or any other Department of this Government.

WILLIAM II. SEWARD, Secretary of State.

The New York papers offered a thousand dollars reward for the discovery of the offending party or parties, and U. S. Marshal Murray was authorized to offer five hundred dollars additional for the messenger who delivered the copies of the bogus proclamation at the offices of the daily papers. But the matter did not rest here.

The papers which had published it were suppressed, and vigorous efforts made to discover its author. These efforts resulted in the apprehension of Joseph Howard, one of the editors of the Brooklyn *Eagle*, a well known literateur in New York. Howard immediately confessed his guilt, and was sent to Fort Lafayette, and the *World* and *Journal of Commerce* having satisfactorily shown they had published it innocently, were released. A few months afterwards Howard was also set at liberty.

Thus ended the history of this famous forgery.

We have now traced Mr. Lincoln's life through a great variety of vicissitudes, and brought it down to the present eventful times.

He is now before the American people for re-election. His record is familiar to them. It contains many errors, many mistakes, many shortcomings, but not one blot.

I. he has erred, it has been from those infirmities which are common to all men. But, strike a fair balance, and there remains to Mr. Lincoln's credit an unfaltering patriotism, clear good sense, unblemished honesty, untiring devotion, and unmistakable earnestness of purpose.

With these merits, which have shed lustre upon his administration during four years of such trial that few public men creditably survive, he stands before the nation which he has preserved through many perils, for its endorsement and its suffrages.

THE END.

www.ingramcontent.com/pod-product-compliance
Lightning Source LLC
Chambersburg PA
CBHW022012050726
47499CB00007BA/2504